Silent Resilience

To Jenny, my love.

Chapter 1

The early morning air at Chateau Dupont carried the faint scent of lavender from the gardens, mingling with the earthy aroma of dew-soaked soil. Marcel stood on the wide stone terrace; a porcelain espresso cup balanced in his hand. He surveyed the vast vineyard below, the neat rows of vines stretching like emerald ribbons across the undulating landscape. It was a sight that never failed to fill him with quiet pride.

As he stood there, a memory stirred in the quiet recesses of his mind—his father's voice, firm yet warm, as he guided a young Marcel through the very same rows.

"Every vine is a promise," his father had said, his weathered hands caressing a budding shoot.

"A promise of hard work, care, and patience. And if we honour that promise, the vineyard will reward us."

Marcel could still see his father, sweat beading on his brow as he laboured under the midday sun, pruning the vines with meticulous precision. Though a man of few words, his father's passion for the land spoke volumes in his actions. His unwavering dedication laid the foundation for the legacy that Château Dupont now carried—a wine of global acclaim, celebrated for its complexity and depth, much like the man who had first cultivated it.

His gaze shifted to the gardens below, where Genevieve often worked. The sight reminded him of his mother, who had been the heart of the vineyard in her own way. She was always among the flowers, her hands stained with soil as she tended to the garden with the same care his father gave to the vines. Together, they had been a team, their love and labour intertwined in every bottle of wine made and every meal produced from her vegetable garden.

Genevieve mirrored his mother's spirit—her quiet strength, her boundless energy, and her devotion to the land. Whether she was perfecting her preservative techniques in the lab or nurturing the vines alongside him, she brought a sense of balance and grace to their shared life. Marcel couldn't help but smile at the comparison, grateful for the enduring legacy of love and partnership that had been passed down through generations.

His mind broke from those precious memories, and he gazed at the mountains as the first rays of sunlight spilt over the distant Alps, casting long shadows across the land. He watched the light play across the vines, the leaves shimmering like jewels. His mind, active as always, was now half in the present and half in the world of ideas—molecular structures, fermentation processes, and the ever-persistent mysteries of the universe.

Genevieve emerged from the kitchen; a tray balanced effortlessly in her hands. The silver glinted in the sunlight, the freshly baked croissants still steaming. She wore a simple linen dress, her dark chestnut hair tied back, but to Marcel, she looked as radiant as the day he'd met her.

"You're up early," she said, her voice as light as the morning breeze.

Marcel raised his cup in a mock toast. "Some mornings, the vineyard calls to me before the coffee does."

Genevieve laughed softly, setting the tray down on the terrace table. "Or maybe it's the memories of your father reminding you to keep working hard," she teased gently, her eyes twinkling.

Marcel chuckled. "Perhaps. He'd certainly approve of your croissants and your tiny vase of lavender from the garden. He always believed that beauty in small details similarly made the wine richer somehow."

Genevieve smiled, resting a hand on his arm. "And he was right. It's those small details that make all the difference."

"And you'll spoil me if you keep this up," Marcel said, setting his cup down, and gesturing at the croissants as she approached.

"Someone has to," she replied with a playful smirk, turning to move the plates from the tray onto the table. She delicately placed the miniature vase of lavender at the centre of the table and continued, "Otherwise, you'd survive on coffee and equations."

He chuckled, pulling out a chair for her. "Equations are far more reliable than croissants."

Genevieve sat, her gaze drifting over the vineyard. She smiled as she took in the beauty of the vineyards, and the valleys beyond, with the sun shining through and the majestic Alps in the background.

"Do you ever think about what we've built here, Marcel? The winery, the family, the life we've created?"

Marcel leaned back, his eyes narrowing as he followed her line of sight. "All the time. It's a legacy. Ours and the children's. A balance of nature and science."

Her smile softened. "And yet, there's always more to discover. Sometimes I wonder if we're meddling too much. If our desire to improve things could... backfire."

He reached for her hand, his fingers brushing hers. "We've dedicated our lives to understanding the world, Genevieve. Not to harm it but to enhance it. Progress requires risk."

Genevieve looked at him, her green eyes searching his face. "But what if the risks outweigh the rewards?"

Marcel didn't answer immediately. He picked up his espresso and took a measured sip, the bitter liquid grounding him. "Then we proceed with caution. But we don't stop."

The gentle clink of a bird's wings against a metal lantern broke the moment. Genevieve tilted her head, watching the sparrow flit away into the vines. "Perhaps you're right. Still, it wouldn't hurt to take a moment to simply enjoy what we've already accomplished."
Marcel smiled, leaning forward to brush a kiss across her knuckles. "Agreed. But only after I check the fermentation tanks."

She laughed, shaking her head. "You're incorrigible."

"And you wouldn't have me any other way," he replied, his eyes twinkling.

Their shared laughter echoed across the terrace, carried by the wind into the heart of the vineyard. It was a picture-perfect morning, the kind that seemed untouchable. But beneath its serenity, life had a way of hiding the tremors before the quake.

* * *

The air in the winery was cool and faintly sweet, carrying the scent of fermenting grapes. Marcel stepped through the large oak doors, the rhythmic hum of machinery and the occasional clinking of metal greeting him like an old friend. Inside, amidst the stainless-steel fermentation tanks that gleamed under soft industrial lights, Jean-Pierre was bent over a clipboard, his brow furrowed in concentration.

"Jean-Pierre," Marcel called, his voice cutting through the quiet.

Jean-Pierre straightened, turning to face his father with a smile. He held a thermometer in one hand, the clipboard tucked under his arm. "*Papa*," he replied warmly. "You're just in time. I was about to check the sulphur levels on the new fermentation."

Marcel approached his curiosity piqued. "Ah, good. How are they looking so far? Acidity, sugars? Everything in balance?"

Jean-Pierre's hazel eyes lit up with enthusiasm. "Better than we hoped. The sugars are holding steady, and the acid profile is nearly perfect. I think this might be one of our best vintages yet."

Marcel leaned over to inspect the bubbling liquid inside the open tank. The faint froth at the surface shimmered in the light, evidence of yeast hard at work. He reached for the clipboard Jean-Pierre offered, scanning the numbers with a critical eye.

"Brix level at 23," Marcel murmured, nodding approvingly. "Excellent start. And the sulphur readings?"

Jean-Pierre moved to a nearby table where a series of small vials sat, each labelled meticulously. He picked one up and held it out. "Just tested. SO2 levels are at 25 parts per million. Still within range."

"Good," Marcel said, the faintest hint of pride creeping into his voice. "But remember, too much sulphur can mask the fruit. Keep it balanced."

Jean-Pierre grinned, his admiration for his father evident. "I know, *Papa*. Balance is everything. You've drilled that into me since I was a boy."

Marcel chuckled, a rare sound that softened his otherwise serious demeanour. "And for good reason. The difference between an average wine and an exceptional one often lies in those tiny details. Just like the cosmos, Jean-Pierre. The smallest particle can produce the biggest change."

They moved together through the winery, discussing the nuances of the fermentation process. Jean-Pierre's passion was evident as he spoke about a new strain of yeast he was experimenting with; one he believed could enhance the floral notes in their white wines.

"I've been researching this yeast for months," Jean-Pierre explained, his excitement infectious. "It's supposed to bring out the citrus and honeysuckle tones without compromising structure. I think it could be a game-changer."

Marcel listened intently, impressed by his son's dedication. "You've always had an eye for innovation," he said. "But remember, tradition has its place too. The vines teach us patience, and the wine teaches us humility. Never lose sight of that."
Jean-Pierre nodded; his expression thoughtful. "I won't, Papa. The vineyard is as much a teacher as it is a legacy."

Chapter 2

Outside, the afternoon sun bathed the Dupont estate in golden light. In a corner of the sprawling gardens, Genevieve knelt among rows of herbs and vegetables, her hands deftly snipping sprigs of rosemary and thyme. Her basket was already brimming with fresh produce, vibrant tomatoes, crisp lettuce, and fragrant basil.

This garden was her sanctuary, a place where the confusion of the world faded, and the simplicity of nature took over. She paused to admire the vibrant green of the parsley leaves, their sharp, fresh scent mingling with the earthy aroma of the soil.

Genevieve stood for a moment, her hands brushing the delicate parsley stems as her thoughts wandered. A gentle smile spread across her face as she reflected on how her journey through science had intertwined seamlessly with her love for nature. Her early studies in chemical compounds, compositions, and reactions sparked a fascination with food quality and preservation. That curiosity had grown into a deeper passion—one that extended beyond the laboratory and into her home, her family, and their vineyard.

It was this very passion that had inspired Jean-Pierre. Genevieve had often marvelled at her son's ability to balance nature's purity with the precision of science. She had encouraged him to see the vineyard as more than just rows of vines to be harvested—it was a living ecosystem, deserving of respect and care. It was her influence that had driven him to seek innovative yet sustainable practices, preserving the land's natural beauty rather than overwhelming it with chemicals.

Her smile deepened as she thought of her kitchen, where shelves were lined with rows of homemade preserves, jams, and pickles, each jar a testament to her dedication. From the garden to the plate, Genevieve believed in honouring nature's bounty, nurturing it to provide not only sustenance but a connection to the earth. Cooking had always been an extension of her love for science— a process of experimenting, balancing, and creating something beautiful.

She reached for another sprig of parsley, her mind already wandering to her next recipe. But more than the dishes she would prepare, she felt a quiet pride in knowing that her work in both science and the vineyard had created a legacy—one that blended innovation with tradition and one that she hoped would endure through her family for generations to come.

For Genevieve, cooking was more than a chore—it was an art, a way to nurture her family and connect with the land. Each meal was a celebration of the flavours they had cultivated together, a testament to the harmony between science and nature that defined their lives.

As she stood, her basket in hand, she envisioned the meal she would prepare that evening. A rustic Provençal stew, rich with the herbs she had gathered, accompanied by a loaf of fresh bread and, of course, a bottle of their finest red.

The thought of bringing her family together around the dinner table filled her with quiet contentment. It was in these moments—when laughter and conversation flowed as freely as the wine—that she felt most at peace.

***

As the sun dipped below the horizon, casting long shadows across the estate, Marcel and Jean-Pierre returned from the winery, their conversation still revolving around yeast strains and barrel ageing. They found Genevieve in the kitchen, her apron dusted with flour as she kneaded dough for the evening's bread.

"Ah, there you are," she greeted them with a smile. "Just in time to set the table."
Jean-Pierre stepped forward, planting a quick kiss on her cheek. "Smells amazing, *Maman*. What's on the menu tonight?"

"A little something inspired by the garden," she replied, nodding toward the basket of herbs and vegetables on the counter.

Marcel inhaled deeply, savouring the aroma. "You've outdone yourself, as always."

Genevieve waved a hand dismissively, though her eyes sparkled with pleasure. "It's nothing fancy. Just good, honest food."

As they worked together to prepare the meal, their conversation turned to Chantelle.

"Her graduation is just a few weeks away," Genevieve said, her voice tinged with pride. "Can you believe it? Our little girl, a doctor."
"She's worked so hard," Marcel said, his tone reflective. "I see so much of you in her, Genevieve. Her determination, her compassion."

Jean-Pierre, who had been setting plates on the table, chimed in. "She's going to be incredible. But I can't help worrying about her. Medicine is a tough field, and she's always pushing herself so hard."

Genevieve placed a reassuring hand on his shoulder. "She's stronger than you think, Jean-Pierre. And she knows she has us to lean on."

Marcel nodded in agreement. "You've always been protective of her, and that's good. But Chantelle is more than capable of taking care of herself. She's proven that time and again."

Jean-Pierre sighed, a small smile playing on his lips. "I know. I just can't help it. She's my little sister."

As the family sat down to dinner, the warmth of their bond was felt by all. They shared stories, laughter, and dreams, the challenges of the day forgotten in the glow of their togetherness.

For Marcel, Genevieve, and Jean-Pierre, the vineyard and the winery were more than a livelihood—they were the heart of their family, a legacy they nurtured not just in the land but in each other.

Chapter 3

The expansive lecture hall was a theatre of anticipation. Hundreds of students, professors, and scientific luminaries filled the room, their murmured conversations a hum of excitement. Above the stage, a colossal screen was suspended, its darkened surface waiting to display the secrets of the cosmos. The walls bore the faint etching of past achievements—equations and diagrams that seemed to whisper of the groundbreaking work done within these hallowed halls.

At the podium stood the dean of the university, his distinguished presence commanding silence as he adjusted his microphone. His gaze swept the room, a smile of pride softening the sharp lines of his face.

"Ladies and gentlemen, it is my great honour to introduce today's speaker," the dean began, his voice resonating with warmth.

"A man whose contributions to astrophysics and science as a whole are unparalleled. Professor Marcel Dupont is not just an academic of the highest order but also a trailblazer whose work at major scientific institutions has deepened our understanding of the universe."

The audience broke into polite applause, though the students in particular were barely able to contain their enthusiasm. Marcel, seated just off-stage, adjusted his glasses and rose, his movements calm but purposeful. The dean gestured toward him.

"Please join me in welcoming Professor Dupont to the stage," the dean concluded, stepping aside to allow Marcel to take the spotlight.

Marcel stepped forward, his commanding yet approachable presence instantly capturing the room. His silver hair glinted in the light, and his tailored suit spoke of a man who valued precision and clarity in all things, not least his appearance. He paused to take in the faces before him, a mixture of young, eager minds and seasoned academics.

"Thank you, Dean Olivier," Marcel began, his voice steady and deliberate, "and thank you all for being here. It's a privilege to address such a distinguished audience."

The applause faded, and the room stilled, every eye fixed on him. Marcel gestured toward the dark screen, which flickered to life behind him. The first image was a breathtaking composite of the universe: galaxies spiralling in vivid colours, nebulae glowing like cosmic flames, and stars strewn across the black void like scattered jewels.

"The universe," Marcel began, his tone imbued with a reverence that made the room lean in, "is a place of intrigue, diversity, and, above all, chaos."

He clicked a remote, and the screen shifted to display a black hole, its event horizon swirling like an endless whirlpool of light and darkness.

"Let's start with chaos," he said. "Black holes are perhaps the ultimate embodiment of it. They are places where the laws of physics as we know them break down—a singularity where gravity is so intense that not even light can escape."

The image morphed into the aftermath of a supernova, a star exploding in a violent dance of death and renewal. "And yet, from this mayhem comes creation," Marcel continued. "The death of a star paves the way for the birth of new elements, new stars, and ultimately, new life."

He moved through slides with effortless precision, each more captivating than the last: pulsars spinning with relentless energy, quasars blazing as the universe's most luminous beacons, and white dwarfs—the remnants of once-mighty stars, now quietly fading.

"Everything in the cosmos," Marcel said, pausing for emphasis, "is interconnected. Disorder and order exist in a delicate balance. From the violence of a supernova to the serene birth of a star, the universe teaches us that destruction and creation are two sides of the same coin."

The screen now displayed a visual representation of particle collisions, streams of matter and antimatter colliding in vivid, chaotic bursts. Marcel's enthusiasm became almost palpable as he gestured toward the image.

He pointed to the aftermath displayed on the screen: a dazzling cascade of particles and energy. "What you see here is a microcosm of the universe's birth—a Big Bang in miniature. In this confusion, we discover the fundamental building blocks of everything."

Marcel paused, his gaze sweeping the room. "It is in the aftermath of this turmoil that we find answers to some of humanity's greatest questions. What are we made of? Where do we come from? And, perhaps, where are we going?"

The audience was enraptured, hanging on his every word. Marcel's tone shifted slightly, growing more introspective.

"But havoc is not confined to the universe or the subatomic realm," he said. "It is present in our lives, in our societies. And just as the universe transforms disorder into order, so too must we. It is in our power to harness the upheavals we face and use them to create something meaningful."

He allowed the words to linger, a subtle hint at the challenges his family—and the world—would soon confront. Yet he did not dwell on the ominous. Instead, he returned to the cosmos, guiding the audience back to the stars.

"Remember this," Marcel concluded, his voice firm but uplifting. "The universe is not static. It is ever-changing, ever evolving. And in its constant motion, it reminds us of one profound truth: that even in the darkest of voids, light is born."

As Marcel stepped back from the podium, the room erupted into thunderous applause. The standing ovation was instantaneous, sweeping across the hall like a wave. Students and seasoned scientists alike rose to their feet, their admiration clear in their bright faces and relentless clapping.

Dean Olivier returned to the stage, his hands clapping enthusiastically. "Ladies and gentlemen," he said, his voice rising above the applause, "Professor Dupont has once again shown us why he is one of the great minds of our time. Let us give him another round of applause."

The ovation continued, Marcel standing modestly to one side, his hands folded in front of him. His sharp mind had already moved on, replaying the connections he had made during the lecture and filing away new ideas sparked by the audience's energy.

As the crowd started to disperse, a young astrophysics student lingered near the podium. Her hands fidgeted with a notebook, her voice quivering with awe as she asked, "Professor, do you think the commotion in the universe mirrors the confusion in human existence?" Marcel's lips curled in a faint smile. "Perhaps," he said, his voice as enigmatic as the stars. "But disorderliness, in its truest form, is merely a precursor to creation." Her mind sparked into thought, perhaps realising the depth that statement carried as she smiled and walked on.

Later, as the lecture hall emptied, Marcel remained behind for a moment. He stood by the podium, gazing at the screen, now dark once more. The stillness of the room contrasted sharply with the vibrancy of the cosmos he had just described.

"Even in confusion," he murmured to himself, "there is a pattern."

Satisfied, he gathered his notes and left the hall, his thoughts already turning to his family, his research, and the chaos yet to come.

Chapter 4

Marcel exited the grand lecture hall, his thoughts still lingering on the applause that followed his presentation. The brisk evening air greeted him, a sharp contrast to the warmth of the crowd inside. He tugged his coat tighter and began his walk back to the hotel, his mind teeming with ideas about the vast cosmos and the mysteries of the universe.

Turning down a quieter street, his footsteps echoed off the cobblestones. The smell of damp concrete mingled with something far less pleasant—alcohol, sweat, and decay. On the corner, a group of vagrants huddled around a flickering streetlamp, their faces gaunt and their eyes hollow.

One man, his hands trembling, clutched a bottle of cheap liquor, while another heated the end of a needle over a makeshift flame. Marcel's stride faltered as he caught sight of the syringe plunging into a bruised vein.

A wave of disgust and sorrow swept over him. How had humanity fallen to this? In a world where the secrets of the stars lay within reach, people still sought solace in self-destruction.

One of the men glanced up, his bloodshot eyes meeting Marcel's gaze for a fleeting moment. There was no recognition, no shame—just a hollow stare that spoke of pain and desperation. Marcel quickened his pace, eager to leave the scene behind, but the image lingered in his mind.

By the time he reached the hotel, he couldn't shake the thought: a world capable of such self-inflicted ruin might not be ready for the discoveries he sought to share.

***

Returning to his hotel after the lecture, Marcel sank into a plush armchair by the window, the lingering echoes of applause still vivid in his mind. Yet, amidst the satisfaction of a successful presentation, the image of the vagrants loitering on the pavement outside the lecture hall tugged at his thoughts. Their gaunt faces, the hollow stares, the telltale signs of needles discarded nearby—it all spoke of lives consumed by addiction and despair.

Marcel poured himself a glass of wine, the rich aroma of the vintage mingling with the crisp evening air drifting through the window. He turned his gaze toward the serene expanse of Lake Geneva, its surface glittering with the reflections of city lights. The universe itself seemed to mirror his thoughts—a vast, complex system capable of both breathtaking beauty and catastrophic imbalance.

His mind wandered to Chantelle. Her upcoming graduation filled him with immense pride, a beacon of hope against the shadows of society's failures. He imagined her stepping into the world as a fully-fledged medical professional, ready to face the harsh realities of addiction, despair, and broken lives. Chantelle had always been passionate, driven by an unrelenting desire to heal and uplift. She possessed a rare combination of empathy and resolve, traits that Marcel admired deeply and knew would serve her well.

He raised his glass in a quiet toast to his daughter, her bright future, and the difference she was destined to make. In the stillness of the moment, he allowed himself to dream—not just of her success but of a world where her efforts, and perhaps even his own, could ripple outward to create lasting change. The stars above seemed to agree, their faint shimmer a reminder of the infinite possibilities life held for those brave enough to reach for them.

Marcel took a contemplative sip of his wine, letting the tranquillity of the lake and the weight of his reflections settle around him. Tonight, he would allow himself this quiet pride, this anticipation of the days to come. Tomorrow, the work would continue—but for now, he savoured the hope that Chantelle's future inspired.

Chapter 5

The grand oak table, polished to a mirror-like sheen, stretched the length of the room, its surface laden with fine china and crystal glasses. The scent of roasted lamb and freshly baked bread wafted through the air, mingling with the faint floral notes of the wine resting in each guest's glass.

Chantelle sat at the centre of attention, her emerald-green dress catching the soft glow of the chandelier above. Her long, dark hair was swept back, revealing a face that was equal parts youthful and composed. The degree she had earned as a newly minted medical doctor rested in a leather-bound case beside her, a symbol of years of dedication and sacrifice.

"To Chantelle," Marcel said, raising his glass in a toast. His deep voice carried the weight of pride and emotion. "For proving that hard work and determination run strong in the Dupont family."

The room erupted in cheers, glasses clinking as everyone joined the toast. Chantelle smiled, though a faint blush coloured her cheeks. "Thank you, Papa," she said softly, her voice steady despite the attention. "But I wouldn't be here without all of you. This is as much your accomplishment as mine."

Genevieve reached across the table, her hand resting gently on Chantelle's. "You've earned every bit of this moment, my darling. And I couldn't be prouder of the woman you've become."

Jean-Pierre, seated beside his sister, leaned back in his chair with an easy grin. "Don't let her fool you," he teased. "She may be a doctor now, but she still can't beat me at tennis."

Chantelle shot him a look, her lips curving into a sly smile. "That's only because you cheat, Jean-Pierre."

The table erupted in laughter, the kind that came easily among family. Marcel watched the exchange with a quiet smile, his heart swelling at the sight of his children. It was moments like this that reminded him why he worked so hard—why he had spent decades building a life that could sustain not just their family but their dreams.

As the meal continued, the conversation shifted from Chantelle's graduation to the winery's latest vintage. Jean-Pierre spoke passionately about the harvest, describing the subtle changes in the soil and climate that had influenced the flavour profile of their newest wine. Chantelle listened with interest, though her thoughts seemed to wander.

Genevieve noticed and leaned in. "You're quiet tonight, darling. Everything all right?"

Chantelle hesitated before nodding. "Just thinking about the hospital. It feels surreal that in a few weeks, I'll be treating patients on my own. What if I'm not ready?"

Marcel's brow furrowed, his gaze settling on his daughter. "You've spent years preparing for this, Chantelle. If anyone is ready, it's you."

Jean-Pierre raised his glass in agreement. "You've got this, little sister. And if you don't, just prescribe wine. Works for me."

Chantelle rolled her eyes, though her smile returned. "Thank you, both of you. I'll try to remember that."

After dessert, the table gradually cleared, and the family moved into the sitting room where a small gathering of friends and colleagues from the scientific community mingled. Some had known Marcel and Genevieve for years, sharing memories of conferences and collaborative research that had shaped their careers. Others were newer acquaintances, drawn to the Dupont estate by its reputation for fine wine and stimulating conversation.

It wasn't long before someone broached the topic of Marcel and Genevieve's upcoming trip to Chornobyl.

"So," began one of the guests, a nuclear physicist named Dr. Alain Perrault, swirling his glass of wine thoughtfully.

"What's this I hear about a research trip? Back in the field after all these years, Marcel?"

Marcel's face lit up, the familiar glimmer of intellectual excitement in his eyes. "Indeed, Alain. It's been too long since I've had the opportunity to do hands-on research. The trip to Chornobyl offers a unique chance to study the effects of nuclear fallout over decades. I'm particularly interested in tracing similarities to the dynamics of gamma-ray bursts and radiation in stellar phenomena—how energy disperses and impacts its surroundings."

Another guest, a younger environmental scientist, leaned in eagerly. "That's fascinating! You're hoping to draw parallels between cosmic radiation and terrestrial nuclear fallout?"

"Exactly," Marcel replied, his tone animated. "Radiation, whether from a supernova or a reactor meltdown, leaves a lasting imprint. Understanding these imprints can deepen our knowledge of both astrophysics and environmental recovery."

Genevieve chimed in, her voice warm and steady. "For me, the focus is more earthbound. I'm curious about how life has adapted in the Exclusion Zone. Nature always finds a way, even in the most extreme circumstances. I'm particularly interested in how plants and fungi have evolved mechanisms to survive in contaminated soil. It could have implications for food preservation and agricultural sustainability."

Dr. Perrault raised an eyebrow. "Food preservation in a nuclear fallout zone? That's certainly ambitious."

Genevieve smiled. "Not as ambitious as you might think. Fermentation, for example, is an ancient method of preservation that thrives on microbial interactions. I'm curious whether those same interactions change in a radioactive environment and what we can learn from that."

"You two make it sound as if this is a vacation," another guest teased, though there was clear admiration in his tone. "Back to the field like the old days, eh?"

Marcel and Genevieve exchanged a look, their smiles tinged with nostalgia.

"In a way, yes," Marcel said. "It reminds us of the days when we were young researchers, driven by pure curiosity. Of course, the stakes are higher now, but the thrill of discovery is the same."

"And the chance to collaborate," Genevieve added. "We've always worked best as a team."

The conversation drifted to memories of past expeditions, each anecdote painting a vivid picture of their shared history. Marcel recounted a night spent under the stars in the Atacama Desert, mapping celestial phenomena, while Genevieve described a particularly challenging study of alpine vegetation in the Swiss Alps.

Their guests listened intently, captivated not only by the stories but also by the evident bond between the two. Marcel's precise, analytical perspective was perfectly complemented by Genevieve's intuitive, holistic approach. Together, they embodied the harmony of science and art, logic and creativity.

As the evening wore on, Marcel and Genevieve's excitement became contagious, sparking a lively discussion about the possibilities of their research. By the time the last guest departed, the room was buzzing with anticipation for their journey.

Marcel poured himself a final glass of wine, his gaze meeting Genevieve's across the room. "It feels good to be doing this again," he said softly.

Genevieve nodded; her expression thoughtful. "It does. It reminds me of why we started in the first place—to ask questions, to seek answers, to leave the world better than we found it."

"And to do it together," Marcel added, raising his glass in a quiet toast.

"To us," Genevieve said, clinking her glass against his.

The moment lingered; a quiet affirmation of their shared purpose and the journey that lay ahead.

And for Chantelle, as the evening wore on, the warmth in the room deepened. Stories were shared, memories revisited, and laughter flowed as freely as the wine. It was a night that seemed untouchable, a celebration of everything the family had worked for.

But even as the candles burned low and the last of the wine was poured, a shadow of unease lingered in Chantelle's mind. She couldn't shake the feeling that her future—so carefully planned—was about to take an unexpected turn.

Mario Zatta

Chapter 6

Before embarking on their research at Chornobyl, Marcel and Genevieve deliberated over the trip's logistics. A direct flight would have been efficient, but it felt devoid of character—too rushed and transactional for what they envisioned. Instead, they chose a slower, more deliberate route, one that mirrored their philosophy of savouring life. Travelling by train would allow them to turn the journey into an excursion, a chance to immerse themselves in the landscapes and cultures that lay between Switzerland and their destination.

The decision was born from their shared passion for travel. They saw it as a way to reconnect with what they loved most—exploring quaint villages, walking cobblestone streets steeped in history, and sampling local delicacies. This wasn't just a detour; it was a necessary pause, a way to feed their curiosity and creativity before diving into the seriousness of their research. With train tickets booked and an itinerary of stops planned, Marcel and Genevieve felt a surge of excitement, knowing that each station promised a new story to unfold.

The rhythmic clatter of the train gave way to an anticipatory quiet as the countryside shifted, revealing rolling hills and charming villages. Marcel and Genevieve gazed out the window, their expressions alight with the thrill of discovery. The train slowed, and the town of Rothenburg ob der Tauber emerged—a fairytale brought to life with its ancient walls, red-tiled roofs, and cobblestone streets.

The crisp autumn air greeted them as they stepped onto the platform, carrying the faint scent of woodsmoke and freshly baked pastries. Marcel adjusted his scarf and smiled. "This place feels like stepping into a storybook."

Genevieve nodded, taking in the timber-framed houses that lined the streets. "Let's see what tales Rothenburg has to share."

Their first destination was the town square, the heart of Rothenburg. The Rathaus, or Town Hall, stood proudly, its Gothic and Renaissance facades speaking of centuries of civic pride. They climbed the Rathaus Tower, the narrow spiral staircase leading to a panoramic view of the town.

From the top, the Tauber River wove through the landscape, and the medieval wall encircled the town like a protective embrace. "It's remarkable," Marcel said, his gaze sweeping across the scene. "To think these walls have withstood the march of time."

Genevieve, ever the historian at heart, pointed to a cluster of houses. "There's a story here about the Master Draught during the Thirty Years' War. Legend says the mayor saved the town by drinking an enormous tankard of wine to impress the invading general."

Marcel chuckled. "That sounds like a challenge I might have taken in my younger days."

The couple wandered along the cobblestone streets, their footsteps echoing softly. Rothenburg's half-timbered houses leaned into one another as if sharing secrets. Flower boxes adorned windows, their vibrant blooms a cheerful contrast to the muted autumn palette.

They entered St. Jakob's Church, a masterpiece of Gothic architecture. The highlight was the Heilig-Blut-Altar, or Altar of the Holy Blood, a breathtaking wood carving by Tilman Riemenschneider. Genevieve marvelled at the intricate details of the Last Supper depicted in the altarpiece.

"Riemenschneider's work captures more than scenes," she said. "It captures emotion, devotion."

Marcel added, "Art like this transcends its time. It's a bridge to the past."

The aroma of roasted meats and spices lured them to a small Gasthaus for lunch. The interior was cosy, with wooden beams overhead and candlelight casting a golden glow.

Genevieve decided on a plate of sauerbraten, slow-braised beef served with red cabbage and dumplings. Marcel opted for bratwurst with sauerkraut and a side of freshly baked pretzels.

"This sauerbraten is incredible," Genevieve said, savouring the tender meat. "The tang of the vinegar marinade is balanced perfectly by the richness of the sauce."

Marcel sipped his stein of local beer and smiled. "The beer is as good as the food. There's an artistry in simplicity."

For dessert, they shared schneeballen—crispy pastry balls dusted with powdered sugar. Genevieve laughed as the flaky treat crumbled in her hands.

"It's messy," she said, "but worth every bite."

As dusk approached, they decided to walk the medieval walls that encircled Rothenburg. The elevated path offered a unique perspective of the town below. Marcel ran his fingers along the cool stone, marvelling at its endurance.

"These walls have seen everything," he said. "War, peace, prosperity, hardship. And yet, they stand."

Genevieve paused to look out at the Tauber Valley, its forests and fields bathed in golden light. "It's a reminder," she said, "of the perseverance of places and people."

Their day ended at the Plönlein, one of Rothenburg's most picturesque spots. The timber-framed house and forked streets looked like they belonged in a painting. Lanterns flickered to life, casting a warm glow on the cobblestones.

They found a quiet bench and sat side by side, watching the town settle into the night. The air was cool, carrying the scent of pine and distant fires.

"Days like this," Marcel said, "remind me why we travel. It's not just the sights, but the stories we find."

Genevieve leaned her head on his shoulder. "And the memories we create together."

Chapter 7

The rhythmic hum of hospital machinery blended with the chaotic chatter of emergency personnel. Chantelle Dupont moved swiftly through the ER, her sharp eyes assessing patients and charts as she directed the staff with calm authority. The night had been unrelenting. Gang-related incidents were escalating, leaving a trail of battered, bloodied victims in their wake.

A nurse approached, her face pale. "Dr. Dupont, we've got another one coming in—multiple stab wounds, suspected gang involvement."

Chantelle nodded. "Prepare trauma room three. Let's stabilise and prioritise imaging." She turned to another nurse. "Keep a close eye on bed five; he's showing signs of internal bleeding."

The scene was becoming all too familiar. Gang wars were spilling over into the public domain, with violence no longer confined to shadowy alleyways but erupting on city streets. Chantelle's mind flashed to the last patient she'd seen, a young man no older than twenty, whose life had been violently cut short. It was hard not to feel the weight of despair as each case unfolded.

Later, during a rare quiet moment, Chantelle leaned against the counter, sipping a lukewarm coffee. Her thoughts drifted to her family. She had always been drawn to medicine out of a desire to make a difference, but the challenges she now faced felt insurmountable. How did one fight against a system so deeply entrenched in corruption and addiction?

***

Far away in the serene expanse of the family's vineyard, Jean-Pierre Dupont was grappling with his own concerns. He stood by the fermentation tanks, watching as the blood-red liquid swirled inside, his mind clouded with unease. The wine industry—so deeply intertwined with the Dupont legacy—was beginning to feel the ripples of a growing underworld influence. Reports of cartel involvement in liquor distribution had surfaced, threatening to tarnish the reputation of artisanal producers.

Jean-Pierre's phone buzzed on the counter. It was a message from an industry associate: *"Rumours spreading about tampered batches hitting the market. Be cautious."*

His jaw tightened as he read. The Dupont name had always stood for excellence, but the idea of their wines being exploited or compromised sent a chill down his spine. He needed to discuss this with Marcel upon his return. The preservation of their legacy required vigilance, and Jean-Pierre was determined to protect what generations of Duponts had built.

***

Meanwhile, in a dimly lit backroom of a nondescript building, Giovanni Russo's sharp eyes scanned the faces around the table. The air was thick with cigarette smoke and tension as he outlined his next move. The preservative pills developed by Genevieve Dupont had been a game-changer in the wine industry, hailed for their ability to enhance the shelf life and quality of wines. Russo, however, saw an opportunity far beyond winemaking.

"We're securing the distribution network," Russo began, his voice low but commanding. "These pills… they're more than just a winemaker's dream. They've got potential in other markets if we can… adapt them."

One of his associates leaned forward. "You think she'll sell?"

Russo smirked. "Everyone's got a price. Besides, she's busy playing scientist. She won't even see us coming."

What Russo didn't know was that Genevieve, far from being complacent, was already deep into her research. The original preservative pills had been a triumph, but she wasn't satisfied. She was on the brink of developing an improved formula, one that could revolutionise the industry yet again. Oblivious to Russo's schemes, she worked tirelessly, driven by a passion for innovation and a desire to leave a legacy as enduring as the wines her family crafted.

***

As the night deepened, the Dupont family—separated by miles but united in purpose—each faced their own battles. Chantelle, fighting to save lives in a hospital overwhelmed by violence. Jean-Pierre, determined to shield their family's name from the encroaching shadows of the underworld. And Genevieve, unknowingly standing at the crossroads of innovation and danger. Little did they know, the threads of their individual struggles were weaving together into a tapestry of challenges that would soon engulf them all.

Chapter 8

The train departed Rothenburg ob der Tauber in the early morning, leaving behind its storybook charm. Marcel and Genevieve settled into their seats, the countryside unfolding before them in orange hues of autumn. Their next destination, Nuremberg, promised a blend of medieval history and modern vibrancy.

Marcel sipped his coffee, a thoughtful expression on his face. "It's fascinating how travel connects us to different times. Rothenburg felt like a step back into the Middle Ages, but Nuremberg will show us another layer of history."

Genevieve nodded; her notebook open in her lap. "I've been reading about the city's role during the Renaissance and the war trials. There's so much to learn."

Arriving in Nuremberg, the couple disembarked into a city alive with activity. The Hauptbahnhof, an architectural blend of neo-Renaissance grandeur and modern efficiency, greeted them with its bustling energy.

Their first stop was the Altstadt, or Old Town, encircled by well-preserved medieval walls. They crossed the Königstor, a historic city gate, and found themselves in a maze of cobblestone streets and half-timbered houses. The aroma of freshly baked pretzels wafted from street vendors, mingling with the crisp air.

It was then, as they passed a newspaper stand, that Marcel's eye caught a bold headline: *Drug Cartels at War*. His steps faltered as the words struck a chord, pulling his thoughts back to the scene outside the lecture theatre—the vagrants, the despair etched in their faces, and the lingering unease it had left. Curious but hesitant to delve deeper, Marcel scanned the first few lines, his stomach tightening at the mention of escalating violence and territorial disputes.

"Is everything alright?" Genevieve asked, noticing his pause.

Marcel folded the newspaper back into place, shaking his head lightly. "Just more chaos in the world," he murmured, his tone subdued. "Let's not let it ruin the day."

As they walked on, the cobblestones uneven beneath their feet, Marcel's thoughts drifted to Chantelle. He knew her work in the hospital brought her face-to-face with the fallout from such conflicts—overdoses, violence, lives shattered by addiction. A pang of worry pressed against his chest, and he silently hoped she wouldn't find herself too close to the storm.

The dominant feature of the skyline was the Kaiserburg, or Imperial Castle, perched on a hill. As they climbed the winding path, Marcel admired the sturdy sandstone walls. "Imagine the emperors who stood here, surveying their realm."

At the top, the panoramic view of Nuremberg sprawled before them. The red-tiled roofs and Gothic spires contrasted with the modern cityscape beyond. Genevieve traced the city's outline with her finger. "This place has witnessed both the rise of empires and the weight of history."

Inside the castle, they explored the Romanesque double chapel and the deep castle well, marvelling at the ingenuity of medieval engineering.

Descending from the castle, hunger led them to a traditional beer garden. The setting was rustic and inviting, with wooden tables beneath sprawling chestnut trees.

They ordered Nuremberg's famous bratwurst—small, flavourful sausages grilled to perfection and served with tangy mustard. Marcel paired his meal with a stein of Franconian beer, while Genevieve opted for a refreshing apfelschorle.

"These sausages are delightful," Genevieve said, savouring the smoky flavour. "The simplicity is what makes them extraordinary."

Marcel raised his glass. "To tradition and taste."

For dessert, they shared lebkuchen, a spiced gingerbread cookie native to Nuremberg. Its warm, aromatic spices lingered on their palates as they strolled through the Hauptmarkt, the main market square, where colourful stalls offered everything from fresh produce to handcrafted goods.

Refreshed by their time in Nuremberg, Marcel and Genevieve boarded the next leg of their journey. The train sped eastward, carrying them toward Dresden, the jewel of Saxony. The landscape shifted from rolling hills to lush forests, the late afternoon sun casting long shadows across the countryside.

Genevieve gazed out the window, her thoughts drifting. "Dresden was called the 'Florence on the Elbe.' It must have been magnificent before the war."

Marcel placed a hand over hers. "And it still is, thanks to its people's tenacity. We'll see how beauty and determination can rebuild a city."

The train arrived at Dresden Hauptbahnhof, an architectural marvel with its grand dome and intricate ironwork. Stepping out into the city, they were immediately struck by its juxtaposition of baroque splendour and post-war modernity.

Their first destination was the Frauenkirche, the Church of Our Lady, a symbol of Dresden's rebirth. Destroyed during World War II and painstakingly reconstructed, the church's sandstone dome gleamed in the sunlight.

Inside, the soft light filtered through the high windows, illuminating the intricately painted ceilings and gleaming white interiors. Genevieve stood in awe. "It's a testament to what humanity can achieve, even after destruction."

Marcel admired the restored organ, its gilded pipes a tribute to the city's musical heritage. "This place doesn't just hold history—it embodies hope."

They continued to the Zwinger Palace, an ornate baroque masterpiece that once hosted court festivals.

The palace's courtyards were framed by galleries adorned with statues of mythological figures.

Genevieve marvelled at the symmetry of the architecture. "Every detail here feels like a celebration of art and culture."

The couple entered the Semper Gallery, home to the Old Masters Picture Gallery. They lingered before Raphael's *Sistine Madonna*, its ethereal beauty leaving them speechless.

As evening fell, they dined at a riverside restaurant overlooking the Elbe. The menu featured Saxon specialities, and they began with potato soup, its creamy texture accented by crispy croutons.

For the main course, they shared Sauerbraten, accompanied by red cabbage and potato dumplings. Marcel savoured the tangy richness of the dish. "This reminds me of the balance in winemaking—layers of flavour, each enhancing the other."

Genevieve sipped her glass of Müller-Thurgau, a local white wine. "And the wine pairs perfectly. There's a simplicity and elegance to it."

Dessert was Quarkkeulchen, sweet potato pancakes dusted with cinnamon sugar and served with apple compote. They savoured each bite as the city lights reflected on the river.

After dinner, they strolled along the Brühl's Terrace, known as the "Balcony of Europe." The Elbe shimmered under the moonlight, and the soft hum of the city surrounded them.

They paused to admire the silhouetted domes and spires, their forms mirrored in the water. Marcel wrapped an arm around Genevieve. "Again, this journey reminds me of why we explore—to find beauty, learn from history, and appreciate the moments we share."

Genevieve leaned into him. "And Dresden has given us all three."

Chapter 9

The train glided smoothly into Poland, leaving behind the baroque charm of Dresden. Marcel and Genevieve sat by the window, captivated by the changing scenery. The rolling hills of Saxony gave way to vast plains dotted with small villages; their red-roofed cottages framed by golden fields.

Genevieve jotted notes in her travel diary, pausing occasionally to point out a picturesque church spire or a flock of storks perched on a rooftop. "Poland has such a pastoral beauty," she said. "It feels like stepping into an old painting."

Marcel leaned back, sipping his coffee. "It's humbling, isn't it? This land has seen so much—kingdoms, wars, rebirths—and yet it remains quietly resilient."

As the train approached Krakow, the countryside gave way to a cityscape steeped in history. The towering Wawel Castle and the spires of St. Mary's Basilica emerged on the horizon, silhouetted against the fading light.

Stepping off the train at Krakow Główny, the couple felt an air of timelessness. The station, a blend of modern efficiency and historic charm, buzzed with travellers. Marcel and Genevieve checked into a boutique hotel near the Old Town, eager to explore the city before nightfall.

Their first destination was Rynek Główny, Krakow's Main Market Square, one of Europe's largest medieval squares. The square was alive with activity—street performers, artists, and locals strolling under the glow of lanterns.

The Cloth Hall stood at the centre; its elegant arches lit by warm light. Genevieve admired its Renaissance architecture. "This was the heart of trade for centuries. Imagine the goods that passed through here—spices, silks, amber."

Marcel gestured toward the basilica nearby. "And there's St. Mary's. Let's take a closer look."

Inside, the couple marvelled at the vibrant blue ceiling dotted with stars and the intricate wooden altarpiece carved by Veit Stoss. Marcel was in heaven. Every detail seemed to tell a story, and the soft echo of their footsteps added to the reverence of the space.

As the night deepened, Marcel and Genevieve sought out a traditional Polish restaurant tucked into a side street. The cosy interior was a blend of rustic charm and elegant details, with wooden beams overhead and embroidered linens on the tables.

They started with *żurek*, a sour rye soup served in a bread bowl, its hearty aroma filling the air. Genevieve savoured the first spoonful, her eyes lighting up. "The tanginess is unexpected but so comforting."

Marcel nodded in agreement, dipping a piece of bread into the creamy broth. "It's a perfect start."

For the main course, Marcel chose *pierogi*, dumplings filled with potato, cheese, and onion, while Genevieve opted for *bigos*, a traditional hunter's stew made with sauerkraut, meat, and spices. The flavours were rich and warming, each bite a testament to Polish culinary heritage.

To accompany their meal, they ordered glasses of Polish vodka infused with flavours of honey and herbs. Marcel raised his glass. "To Krakow—a city of history, tenacious durability, and incredible food."

They ended the meal with *sernik*, a creamy Polish cheesecake, and sipped on hot black tea infused with raspberry syrup. The warmth of the meal and the soft hum of conversation around them created a perfect end to their evening.

Before retiring for the night, Marcel and Genevieve took a leisurely walk through the Old Town. The illuminated streets carried a serene quietness, and the night air was crisp and fragrant with the scent of chestnuts roasting at a nearby stall.

They paused at Wawel Hill, looking up at the majestic castle. Marcel smiled. "Each place we visit adds a layer to our understanding of the world, doesn't it?"

Genevieve nodded, wrapping her arm through his. "And it reminds me how much we've yet to see."

The next morning, with hearts full of Krakow's charm, they boarded their train, ready for the next leg of their journey. Poland had welcomed them with open arms, leaving behind memories of its beauty, flavours, and history.

They felt happy, warm, and re-energised. They were now ready and inspired for the research work ahead of them.

Mario Zatta

Chapter 10

The train glided smoothly through the Ukrainian countryside, its rhythmic clatter punctuated by the occasional whistle as it approached a station. Marcel leaned against the window, the glass cool beneath his temple. Outside, he imagined the landscape unfolding like a pastoral painting with rolling fields of sunflowers swaying in the breeze, interspersed with dense clusters of birch and oak trees. Now, however, the remnants of sunflower stalks stood as skeletal sentinels in the frost-covered fields, their bowed heads a silent testament to seasons past.

He found himself silently comparing the scene to the view from earlier on the ride through the Alps. There, the rugged majesty of snow-capped peaks seemed to stretch endlessly into the heavens, a reflection of the unyielding determination of the land itself. Here, the countryside felt softer, more yielding, as he envisioned the golden fields blanketing the earth like a warm embrace. The Alps were stoic and eternal, yet these fields were stark and laden with frost. He could imagine this land seeming alive with movement—fields rippling in the wind; leaves trembling with energy, and bursts of colour breaking the horizon. Yet both carried a quiet serenity, though of vastly different kinds. The Alps whispered of permanence and solitude, while this countryside sang of fleeting beauty and the cycles of life.

Genevieve sat opposite him; a notebook open on her lap. She scribbled notes, her pen moving in deliberate strokes. Her emerald-green eyes occasionally lifted to meet Marcel's hazel gaze, a flicker of shared anticipation passing between them.

"What are you contemplating?" she asked softly, breaking the silence.

Marcel hesitated. "About how peaceful it looks out there," he said, gesturing to the endless expanse of frosted fields and silver birches. "And how deceptive that peace is. We're heading toward a scar on this earth."

Genevieve tilted her head, studying him. "Nature doesn't dwell on scars. It heals. Perhaps that's what we'll find—resilience."

Marcel let her words settle, their optimism mingling with the thoughts already swirling in his mind. His gaze returned to the countryside, but his mind drifted far beyond it—to the vast reaches of the cosmos, where serenity and disorganisation coexisted in perfect tension.

"The universe," he began, his voice quieter now, "is much the same. On one hand, there's a kind of tranquil beauty to it—nebulae blossoming like distant gardens, galaxies spinning in silent, timeless grace. But it's also a theatre of unimaginable violence. Stars die in explosions that outshine entire galaxies, black holes consume everything in their path, and yet, in that madness, new stars are born. Order emerges from disorder, beauty from destruction."

He turned to Genevieve, a small, contemplative smile tugging at his lips. "What you said about nature not dwelling on scars—that's the cosmos too. It doesn't

mourn its supernovae or its collapsing stars. It just…
continues. Rebuilding, reshaping. Resilient."

Genevieve leaned back slightly, her notebook resting on
her lap as she considered his words. "It's a comforting
thought, in a way. That even in destruction, there's
renewal. Maybe that's what we're meant to take from
all this."

Marcel's gaze returned to the fields. The sunflower
stalks, standing resolute despite the wind, seemed like
tiny echoes of the cosmos' defiant persistence. "It's
true," he murmured. "Even here, in the stillness of this
countryside, there's a reminder of that balance—tumult
and tranquillity. These fields, this earth—it bears the
marks of history, just like the universe does. And yet, it
endures."

He gestured toward the silver birches in the distance,
their slender trunks gleaming in the morning light.
"Those trees—they remind me of pulsars, standing tall
and steady, marking the passage of time. And the
sunflowers—they're like the stars themselves, once

burning brightly, holding everything together and now burnt out."

Genevieve smiled, her emerald eyes brightening with the shared metaphor. "And here we are, two tiny beings on this vast earth, daring to make sense of it all."

Marcel chuckled softly. "Daring, indeed." He reached over, resting a hand briefly on hers. "But it's worth it. To understand, even a little, is to find our place in the confusion."

Genevieve's expression grew thoughtful. "Maybe that's what resilience really is—finding harmony in the disorganisation. Not erasing the scars but embracing them as part of the story."

Marcel nodded, the weight of their shared purpose settling in his chest like an anchor. "Perhaps Chornobyl is a scar, but it's also a reminder of what we must strive for. Not just answers but understanding—and maybe even redemption."

The train's rhythmic clatter filled the silence that followed, a steady counterpoint to their reflections. The frozen fields and birches continued to blur past the window, a landscape both tranquil and alive, mirroring the cosmos Marcel so often pondered.

For a moment, he closed his eyes, letting the soothing cadence of the train merge with the thoughts cascading through his mind. When he opened them again, Genevieve's gaze met his, a flicker of shared anticipation passing between them. Whatever awaited them in Chornobyl, they would face it together, drawn by the same unrelenting pull of curiosity and hope.

The train slowed as it approached a smaller station, and a cluster of wooden houses with colourful roofs came into view. Villagers waved as they passed, children running along the tracks. The contrast struck Marcel again: life here seemed untouched, yet they were only hours away from one of the most devastating human-made disasters in history.

***

The guide met them at the checkpoint, a tall man with sun-weathered skin and piercing grey eyes. He introduced himself as Ivan, a local scientist who had spent years studying the zone.

"Welcome to Chornobyl," Ivan said, his voice carrying the weight of a place steeped in tragedy. "Before we proceed, I'll need you to put these on."
He handed them thin white coveralls and Geiger counters. The devices emitted faint, irregular clicks, a constant reminder of the invisible menace surrounding them.
"Stay close," Ivan instructed as they entered the Exclusion Zone. "This place has its rules, even if they're not written down."

Around them, crumbling buildings stood like monuments to a forgotten era, their windows black voids gazing out at the wilderness creeping in. The air carried a metallic tang, sharp and unwelcoming, mingled with the faint, earthy scent of moss reclaiming the asphalt."

The drive through the zone was haunting. Trees lined the road, their gnarled branches reaching out like skeletal hands. Wild grasses and mosses spilt over cracked asphalt, reclaiming the land. Both Genevieve and Marcel sat silently, taking it all in but Genevieve's mind was a whirl of conflicting thoughts as she gazed out the window. The forest seemed caught in a paradox—eerily lifeless yet teeming with an odd kind of vitality. She noted the tufts of moss carpeting the shattered pavement and the delicate vines curling around rusted signposts. Even in the shadow of devastation, life was pushing forward, adapting, and reclaiming what was lost.

Nature's tenacity, she thought, her scientific curiosity mingling with a pang of sorrow. Her research had always revolved around preservation, finding ways to extend the life of what was valuable—wine, produce, even the fragile bonds of human existence. Now, confronted with this strange, defiant rebirth, she felt a renewed urgency. If nature could find a way to thrive here, in this scarred and poisoned land, then perhaps her work could have a similar impact.

Across from her, Marcel's expression was inscrutable, his hazel eyes narrowed as he stared at the passing scenery. His thoughts travelled outward, far beyond the confines of the Exclusion Zone. He saw in the twisted branches and decaying infrastructure a reflection of the universe itself—a system governed by cycles of destruction and creation. To him, this place was like a supernova remnant: the aftermath of an immense, catastrophic event, yet one that seeded the potential for renewal.

Disorder and order, he mused, his analytical mind working to make sense of it all. He thought of radiation, both as a destructive force and as a tool of discovery—one he had wielded in his work to unveil the mysteries of existence. Here, it had left its indelible mark on the earth, mutating life and transforming landscapes. Marcel couldn't help but wonder: was it possible to truly harness such power for good? Could humanity ever control the mayhem it created, or was it destined to stumble through its own destruction?

Ivan, seated beside Marcel, cast a quick glance at the two of them as if trying to decipher their thoughts. He had guided many researchers through this desolate zone, each one arriving with their own agendas and preconceptions. But Marcel and Genevieve were different—there was a quiet intensity to them, a shared sense of purpose that intrigued him.

For Ivan, the Exclusion Zone was no longer just a place. It was a living, breathing entity, one that had learned to endure despite its wounds. As a scientist, he marvelled at how nature had adapted to radiation levels that would have been fatal to most living things elsewhere. Birds nested in the hollowed-out buildings, wild boars roamed freely through the abandoned streets, and resilient plants thrived where human life had been extinguished.

"It looks dead," Ivan said aloud, breaking the silence, "but it's alive. Nature has found ways to adjust, to regrow. This land doesn't forget what happened, but it moves on. It adapts."

Genevieve turned to him; her expression thoughtful. "It's remarkable. And humbling. This… regrowth, it's not just survival—it's reinvention."

Ivan nodded, his weathered face softening into a faint smile. "It's a reminder, isn't it? That life doesn't need us. It carries on, whether we help it or harm it. The question is, what role do we choose to play?"

Marcel's voice was quiet but firm. "The role of understanding. Of finding answers before our ignorance leaves scars like this elsewhere."

The car slowed as they passed a crumbling building, its windows shattered, its walls streaked with the patina of time and decay. Ivy crept up its facade, reaching toward the roof like a silent conqueror.

"Even here," Marcel murmured, "there's beauty. It's not the kind of beauty we like to admire, but it's there. Nature's relentless determination to reclaim and repurpose—it's extraordinary."

Ivan gestured toward the horizon, where the skeletal remains of a Ferris wheel rose against the sky like a grim monument. "And yet, not everything can be reclaimed. Some things—some memories—linger like ghosts. You'll see soon enough."

The three of them fell silent, each lost in their thoughts as the car continued its slow journey through the zone. The landscape outside shifted subtly, from dense forest to open clearings scattered with fragments of human life—abandoned toys, rusting bicycles, forgotten signs of the past.

For Genevieve, each object felt like a whisper from history, a reminder of lives interrupted, and dreams left unfinished. For Marcel, the scenery was a stark illustration of humanity's fragility, a visual metaphor for the thin line between progress and catastrophe. And for Ivan, it was simply home—a strange, haunting home that bore witness to both the worst and the best of human perseverance.

***

When they reached the outskirts of **Pripyat**, the abandoned city loomed before them. The silence was deafening, broken only by the distant call of a bird or the rustle of leaves in the breeze.

Marcel stepped out of the car, the air heavy with an unplaceable scent—damp earth and decay. He stared at the Ferris wheel, its bright yellow seats now rusted and hanging at odd angles. The sight felt like a grim memorial to lives interrupted.

Marcel stood frozen for a moment; his feet rooted to the ground as if the gravity of the place itself held him still. His eyes wandered from the crumbling Ferris wheel to the overgrown pathways and abandoned structures, each one a haunting reminder of life suspended in time. He tried to reconcile what he was seeing with the serene landscapes he knew so well back home—the whispering forests of the Alps, their quiet stillness brimming with life.

In the Alps, silence was a refuge. It was the gentle rustle of wind through pines, the distant sound of a brook, and the harmonious rhythm of a world thriving in balance. Here, the stillness was different. It was heavy, oppressive, and unnatural, as though the land itself held its breath in mourning. Even the trees seemed to grow cautiously, their branches twisted and sparse, reaching out like tentative fingers toward a sky that had once rained devastation.

Marcel's scientific mind kicked into overdrive, dissecting the tableau before him. He scanned the rusting metal, the jagged edges of broken windows, and the cracks splitting the concrete. His thoughts drifted to radiation—the invisible force that had seeped into every corner of this place, altering its DNA. The very molecules of life had been twisted and warped, yet nature persisted.

He tilted his head, his gaze following a sapling that had pushed its way through a fissure in the asphalt. How did it manage to grow here, in soil laced with poison? What mechanisms allowed it to adapt and survive when the odds were so firmly stacked against it? His thoughts darted to his own work, to the countless hours spent analysing data and experimenting with formulas. If there was a lesson to be learned here, he was determined to find it.

Marcel closed his eyes for a brief moment, imagining the lush greenery of the Alps, their order and tranquillity. Then he opened them again to the havoc before him. This place wasn't just a scar—it was a paradox, a reminder of destruction and survival existing side by side. His mind raced with questions, theories, and connections, trying to piece together the story this land was telling.

"Marcel," Genevieve's voice broke through his thoughts, soft but grounding. He turned to see her watching him, her eyes filled with a mixture of curiosity and concern.

"Just... trying to take it all in," he murmured.

She nodded, understanding without needing further explanation. Together, they stood in the shadow of the Ferris wheel, two scientists in a graveyard of human ambition, each searching for meaning in the confusion.

Genevieve wandered a few steps ahead, pausing to inspect a patch of wildflowers that had forced their way through cracks in the concrete. "It's beautiful in its own way," she murmured. "Life always finds a way."

Marcel followed her gaze, noting how nature had crept into every crevice. Birch trees grew inside abandoned apartment buildings, their roots tangling with shattered glass and debris. A fox darted across the street; its red fur vivid against the grey backdrop.

"Resilience," Marcel echoed her earlier word, but his tone was laced with unease. "But at what cost?"

***

Their final stop was the infamous Red Forest, once a dense pine forest that bore the brunt of the radioactive fallout. Ivan led them carefully along a path, the Geiger counters clicking furiously.

The forest was eerily quiet. The few trees that stood were stunted and twisted; their bark scarred. Yet amidst the desolation, Marcel noticed saplings sprouting defiantly from the soil.

"Nature doesn't give up," Ivan said, noticing Marcel's gaze. "But it doesn't forget either. The radiation is still here, even if you can't see it."

Marcel bent down, running a hand over the wild grasses. They felt coarse, almost brittle. He straightened, glancing at Genevieve, who stood transfixed by the scene. Turning to Ivan, Marcel gestured at the landscape. "Why is it all red?"

Ivan smiled faintly, clearly savouring the opportunity to share his knowledge. He raised his arm, gesturing toward the trees that stretched endlessly into the horizon, their bare, russet branches reaching skyward like frozen flames. "It wasn't always this way," he began, his voice steady and laced with a scientist's precision.

"Before the explosion, this was a thriving pine forest. Vibrant greens, teeming with life. But when the reactor blew, it released a torrent of radiation—cesium-137, strontium-90, iodine-131. The trees here absorbed the brunt of it. The radiation was so intense it killed the pines almost instantly; their chlorophyll was destroyed, and their cells ruptured. Without chlorophyll, they couldn't photosynthesize and couldn't survive. Their needles turned red, like a vast autumn frozen in time."

Genevieve moved closer, her gaze darting from tree to tree, taking in their skeletal forms. "And yet it remains," she said softly.

Ivan nodded, his expression growing more sombre. "Yes, because nature, while fragile, is also incredibly stubborn. The forest has shifted over time. The original pines are long gone, but other plants—grasses, mosses, shrubs—they've started reclaiming the soil, adapting to the contamination. The trees you see now are a mixture of those that withstood the initial blast and those that came later, finding ways to survive despite the odds."

Marcel's face looked studious as he took a step forward, his boots crunching against the dry undergrowth. "So, this redness... it's a remnant of that initial devastation?"

"Exactly," Ivan replied. "A scar left by radiation, etched into the very fabric of this ecosystem. But what's fascinating—and tragic—is that the radiation didn't just kill. It transformed. Mutations, stunted growth, changes in reproduction. Life here has had to rewrite its own rules."

Genevieve crouched, running her fingers over a patch of moss clinging to the base of a tree. "It's haunting," she murmured. "But beautiful in its own way. Like the land is trying to heal itself, even if it never fully can."

Ivan crossed his arms, looking at her with a faint smile. "That's one way to see it. The Red Forest is a symbol of resilience—and fragility. It reminds us of the price of our mistakes, but also of the tenacity of life."

Marcel stared into the distance, where the fiery hues of the forest blurred into the misty horizon. His mind churned with the paradox Ivan described: a place that was both graveyard and cradle, destruction and rebirth intertwined.

"Have you seen any wildlife here?" Marcel asked, breaking the reflective silence.

Ivan nodded. "Oh yes. Wolves, deer, boars, even eagles. They've returned, as if nothing happened. And yet..." He hesitated, his eyes narrowing slightly. "They carry the scars too. Genetic anomalies, shorter lifespans. But they thrive, at least for now. It's a delicate balance."

Marcel turned to Genevieve, who had stood and was watching the trees sway in the light breeze. "You were right," he said softly. "Nature doesn't dwell on scars. It just keeps going, finding a way."

Genevieve met his gaze, her expression thoughtful. "It makes you wonder what lessons we're supposed to learn from all this."

Ivan, who had been quiet for a moment, spoke up with a dry chuckle. "The lesson? That humans are a part of this too. No matter how much damage we do, we're not separate from nature. We're just another species trying to survive in the turmoil we create."

As they continued through the forest, the air seemed to grow heavier, the silence more profound. Yet, beneath the weight of the past, there was an undeniable sense of life—a stubborn, unrelenting will to endure.

Marcel turned to look behind him sensing that Genevieve had stopped.
"What are you thinking?" he asked, echoing her earlier question.

Genevieve turned to him, a faint smile playing on her lips. "That scars tell stories. And sometimes, they hold answers."

Marcel frowned, sensing a deeper meaning in her words. But before he could press her further, Ivan called them back to the vehicle.

Marcel lingered for a moment as Genevieve followed Ivan toward the vehicle, her words still echoing in his mind. His gaze swept over the eerie landscape of the Red Forest, its haunting beauty stirring something deep within him. The stunted, misshapen trees and strange hues of the foliage seemed like a warning, a physical manifestation of the unseen forces that had wreaked havoc here.

As he began to walk back, his steps slowed, weighed down by a troubling thought. He stopped, turning to look once more at the surreal forest. "Genevieve," he called softly, his voice tinged with hesitation.

She paused by the vehicle, catching the tone in his voice. "Yes, Marcel?" she asked, walking back toward him.

He met her eyes, the weight of his thoughts etched into his expression. "Standing here, seeing this… it makes me wonder if anything I've done in my career—any of my discoveries—has caused harm like this. What if my work, my passion for pushing boundaries, has indirectly led to something destructive? What if I've—"

"Marcel," Genevieve interrupted gently, placing a hand on his arm. "You're questioning your legacy, and that's natural. But let me ask you this—did you come here to dwell on fears, or to find solutions?"

He looked at her, his lips pressing into a thin line. "It's not that simple. Standing here, it's impossible not to think about the unintended consequences of science. The Red Forest… it's a reminder of how fragile everything is."

Genevieve followed his gaze, her expression softening. "Yes, it's a scar—a deep one. But even scars tell stories, don't they? This forest is still here. Damaged, yes, but alive. The radiation didn't erase it; it reshaped it. You of all people should know that. You're the one always telling me how the universe reshapes."

She paused, her voice growing thoughtful. "Think of the towns we just visited—Nuremberg, Dresden, Kraków. Each of them was scarred by war and destruction, but they didn't disappear. They rebuilt, stronger, more vibrant. Just like nature does. This forest, those cities— they remind us that even in the face of devastation, there's resilience. Renewal. Transformation."

Marcel's expression softened as her words took hold, the weight in his chest easing slightly. "You always manage to find the light in the darkest places, don't you?"

She smiled. "I just see things as they are, *mon cher*. You've always sought answers in the stars, in the universe's vast expanse. But sometimes, the answers are right here, on the ground. You've taught me that every challenge is an opportunity. Don't let doubt cloud your vision now."

Marcel nodded, taking a deep breath as her words sank in. "You're right. Standing here, I see the scars, but I also see the lessons. Maybe this isn't about what's been lost, but what can still be saved."

Genevieve squeezed his arm, her smile encouraging. "Exactly. And that's why we're here—not to dwell on what we can't change, but to focus on what we can."

As they turned and walked back to the vehicle, Marcel found his stride a little lighter. The Red Forest, with its strange beauty and resilience, no longer felt like a warning. Instead, it seemed like a message—a reminder that even in the shadow of destruction, there was hope. Renewal was possible if only one dared to seek it.

***

That night, they stayed in a modest dormitory in **Chornobyl Town**, its bare walls and simple furnishings a stark contrast to the luxurious comfort they were used to.

Marcel sat by the window, looking out at the distant silhouette of the reactor. He thought of the train ride, the serene landscapes now seeming like a distant dream.

Genevieve joined him, a glass of wine in hand. "To recovery, tenacity and durability," she said, raising her glass.

Genevieve swirled the wine in her glass, watching the liquid catch the dim light of the dormitory. Marcel's toast had struck a chord. "Recovery, tenacity, and durability," she repeated softly, almost to herself. The words settled into her mind like seeds finding fertile soil.

She leaned back in her chair, her gaze drifting past Marcel to the darkened outline of the reactor in the distance. It was a place of devastation, yet even here, life had found a way to endure. The thought struck her deeply, reminding her of her purpose.

She closed her eyes for a moment and let the memories come. The years she had spent in the lab flashed before her—countless hours poring over experiments, testing and retesting, driven by the pursuit of perfection. Those efforts had culminated in the creation of her preservation pills, a groundbreaking innovation that transformed not only her family's wines but also revolutionized the global wine industry. The pills, compact and precise, had become the gold standard for preserving the delicate balance of flavour, aroma, and longevity in wines.

Genevieve's contributions had elevated Chateau Dupont to a position of international acclaim. Their wines now graced the tables of presidents, royalty, and collectors. She had achieved so much, but standing here on the edge of the Exclusion Zone, she felt the stirrings of something greater—a calling to refine her work, to draw inspiration from the forces of nature that thrived against all odds.

Her thoughts turned to Jean-Pierre. Her son had always been attuned to the land, to the rhythms of the vines and the subtleties of the soil. He shared her passion for preservation but viewed it through a lens of stewardship and legacy. She could still hear his voice from their last conversation before this journey:

"It's not just about making good wine, Maman. It's about leaving the land better than we found it, preserving it for the future."

Jean-Pierre's vision had struck a chord in her heart. She wanted her research to go beyond preservation for commerce. She wanted it to align with his philosophy, to honour the land and its capacity to endure and adapt. This trip to Chornobyl wasn't just about studying the effects of radiation on organic compounds; it was about learning from the resilience—and adaptability—of life itself.

Her eyes opened, and she glanced at Marcel, who was still gazing out the window, lost in his own reflections. She marvelled at his ability to see the world through the lens of the universe, to find connections between the macrocosm of the stars and the microcosm of their existence.

"Marcel," she said softly, breaking the silence, "what do you see when you look out there?"

He turned to her, his hazel eyes thoughtful. "I see a paradox," he said after a moment. "A world that is both broken and healing. Out there is a testament to destruction, but also to the quiet determination of life to carry on. It's the same paradox I see in the cosmos—mayhem and creation, destruction and renewal, endlessly intertwined."

She nodded, absorbing his words. "That's why I'm here," she said. "To learn from that paradox. If nature can find a way to adapt and preserve life in a place like this, imagine what we can learn and apply to the world we live in."

Marcel smiled faintly. "You've always had a gift for drawing lessons from the land. From the vineyards to the lab, you see connections most people overlook."

Genevieve felt a flush of warmth at his words. She sipped her wine and stared out at the shadowed outlines of the distant trees, thinking of how even here, in the most unlikely of places, wild grasses and stubborn saplings were claiming the landscape.

"Jean-Pierre would be fascinated by this place," she said. "It's a living example of what he talks about—how nature preserves itself, even after unimaginable devastation. I wonder what he'd make of these forests."

"He'd probably be out there with his soil samples and his notebook," Marcel said, chuckling. "The boy is a Dupont through and through. Always curious, always grounded in the earth."

Genevieve laughed softly. "And Chantelle would have questions about how the mutations affect life forms, no doubt."

The mention of their daughter brought a moment of quiet reflection. Chantelle's analytical mind and medical training had been invaluable in understanding the human element of their work. She approached problems with a discipline that reminded Genevieve of herself at that age, though Chantelle's focus on the human condition often provided a perspective that grounded their scientific pursuits.

Marcel leaned back in his chair, stretching slightly. "It's strange, isn't it? How our family's work, each in our own way, revolves around preservation—whether it's preserving life, preserving the land, or preserving knowledge."

"It's our legacy," Genevieve said simply. "And it's why we're here—to make it stronger, to push it forward."

The two sat in companionable silence for a moment, their thoughts intertwining like the branches of the trees outside.

Ivan's footsteps echoed softly down the hall, a reminder of their location and purpose. Marcel glanced at his wife, a glimmer of pride and determination in his eyes.

"Tomorrow, we'll see just how much this place has to teach us."

Genevieve raised her glass again, her voice steady. "To the lessons we learn, the legacies we build, and the strength to see it through."

Marcel clinked his glass lightly against hers, the sound a small, hopeful note in the quiet dormitory. Outside, the wind whispered through the trees, carrying with it the promise of discovery and the enduring power of life.

Genevieve swirled the wine in her glass, her thoughts returning to the first glimpses of Chornobyl's eerily desolate landscapes. At first, she had been struck by the devastation—a stark reminder of human error and its catastrophic consequences. But as the hours passed and the land unfolded before her, she began to see something else: opportunity and hope.

She thought of the grasses pushing through cracked asphalt, the wildflowers blooming defiantly in radioactive soil, and the creatures that had adapted to live in an environment once deemed uninhabitable. Nature's ability to endure, to find a way to thrive against impossible odds, filled her with awe.

For Genevieve, this was more than a scientific mission—it was a chance to understand the mechanisms of survival on a fundamental level. If she could learn how nature preserved life here, perhaps she could take that knowledge and apply it to her own research. The preservation pills she had created had already revolutionized winemaking, but she wanted to go further. She wanted to craft something that not only prolonged the life of wine but also mirrored the elegance and resilience of nature itself.

As she sipped her wine, she thought of the legacy she was building, one rooted in Jean-Pierre's vision of sustainability and Chantelle's drive to better the human condition. This trip to Chornobyl felt like a convergence of all those ideals, and she felt an eager anticipation stirring within her. Tomorrow, the work would begin—the real work, delving into the mysteries of a land that had refused to surrender to destruction.

She glanced at Marcel, who was still gazing out at the distant reactor, lost in thought. His analytical mind would dissect the science, the data, and the anomalies, while she would seek the connections and inspirations that bridged the gap between devastation and regeneration.

"I'm ready," she said softly, more to herself than to Marcel. Her voice carried a quiet determination, the kind that came from knowing that even in a place as scarred as this, there was something valuable to uncover. Nature had not given up, and neither would she.

Tomorrow, she thought, would be the first step in a journey not just of scientific discovery, but of understanding the deeper truths about life, survival, and the unyielding strength of the natural world.

Marcel hesitated, then clinked his glass against hers knowing they were ready. But as he sipped, he couldn't shake the feeling that resilience came at a cost—and that they were only beginning to uncover the layers of it.

Chapter 11

The next morning, the mist hung low over the Exclusion Zone, shrouding the landscape in an ethereal haze. Marcel and Genevieve arrived at a modest research facility on the edge of Chornobyl Town, its utilitarian concrete structure blending into the sombre surroundings. The facility had been retrofitted from an old administrative building, with sparse but functional equipment humming under the fluorescent lights.

The laboratory was divided into two main sections: one for Marcel and one for Genevieve.

Marcel adjusted the controls on a spectrometer, studying the molecular degradation in a sample exposed to gamma radiation. His thoughts drifted to the cosmos—how the violent forces shaping the early universe had parallels here. Radiation, a primal force, was both a creator and destroyer.

His mind wandered to a lecture he'd once given on nucleosynthesis, the cosmic process that forged the elements in stars. He murmured to himself, "In the confusion, there's order. Even in destruction, there's the promise of creation." He smiled to himself as he remembered the standing ovation he received.

"I hope you're not talking to the molecules again," Genevieve teased, appearing at the doorway with a clipboard.

Marcel glanced up, smirking. "Just contemplating how radiation reshapes everything—atoms, life, even our understanding of the universe."

Genevieve smiled, her gaze lingering on him. "And here you are, trying to unravel it all."
She paused as she admiringly looked at him and then continued, "It reminds me of our uni days. Remember how we unravelled everything together, *mon cher*."

Marcel chuckled, his eyes softening with nostalgia. "How could I forget? Those endless afternoons on the lawns. You, with your coloured pens, mapping out every theory like it was a treasure map. Me, scribbling equations in the margins of your notebooks, trying to connect the dots."

Genevieve leaned against the doorframe, her clipboard resting lightly in her arms. "And the debates," she added, her voice warm. "You were always so sure of your theories, and I'd poke holes in them just to see if you'd catch on."

Marcel laughed, the sound rich and unguarded. "You didn't just poke holes; you tore them wide open. But you were usually right."

"Usually?" she teased, arching a brow. "I seem to recall more than a few all-nighters where you ended up agreeing with me."

He nodded, a fond smile tugging at his lips. "True. Those nights were something else—sitting under the stars, trying to untangle the universe while everyone else was at the pub."

Genevieve's gaze grew distant as she remembered those moments. The cool grass beneath them, the smell of spring in the air, the soft murmur of other students in the distance. She could still see the way Marcel's eyes lit up when he explained a concept, the passion that drew her to him as much as his brilliance. "It wasn't just the theories," she said quietly. "It was how you made me see the world differently. Bigger. Full of possibilities."

Marcel looked at her, his expression tender. "And you grounded me. Made me realize that all the possibilities in the world mean nothing if you don't have someone to share them with."

Genevieve stepped closer, setting the clipboard down on the edge of the desk. She reached out, brushing a stray hair from his forehead. "And here we are," she said softly, her voice steady yet filled with emotion. "Trying to unravel it all again."

Marcel took her hand in his, holding it gently. "Some things never change," he said, his voice a low murmur. "Except now, the stakes feel higher. But with you by my side, Genevieve, I feel like we can face anything."

They stood there for a moment, a quiet understanding passing between them. The room, once filled with the hum of Marcel's musings and the scrape of Genevieve's pen, now held only the shared silence of two people who had spent a lifetime unravelling mysteries—together.

***

Genevieve moved on to the greenhouse, where she sat down and examined a batch of radio trophic fungi—organisms thriving on radiation. She compared their growth patterns to a new strain of genetically modified wheat. Her hypothesis was bold: could the adaptive mechanisms of these plants and fungi inspire preservatives that extended the life of food?

She picked up a notebook and jotted down observations. Her thoughts turned philosophical. Nature was relentless, adapting to the harshest environments. If she could channel that resilience into preservation, it would be transformative—not just for food but for medicine, even survival in space exploration.

"Nature doesn't just endure," she whispered to herself. "It innovates."

The idea thrilled her, sparking a cascade of thoughts. She imagined the possibilities: preservation methods that could keep food fresh for months on end, reducing global waste and ensuring sustainable resources for areas plagued by scarcity. She pictured medical applications, where the same principles could prolong the potency of life-saving drugs in remote or disaster-stricken areas. Could this research eventually enable long-term missions in space, ensuring survival in environments as harsh as the moon or Mars?

"Marcel would like that," she smiled to herself.

Her mind wandered back to Jean-Pierre and his relentless passion for the winery. She envisioned a new era for their family business—wines preserved with natural methods, free from synthetic additives but able to retain their richness and character for decades. It wasn't just about preservation; it was about authenticity. She could already see Jean-Pierre's face light up at the prospect, his quiet intensity giving way to a rare smile as they discussed how these innovations could elevate the legacy of Chateau Dupont.

And then there was Chantelle. Her daughter's determination to make a difference in the medical world always inspired her. Genevieve thought of the countless challenges Chantelle spoke of—fragile vaccines requiring constant refrigeration, medicines degrading before they reached those in need. What if this research could change that? What if she could contribute to solutions that Chantelle could one day implement, saving lives with the same principles that preserved a bottle of their finest wine?

A warmth spread through her chest at the thought of her family, each pursuing their passions with such purpose. For all the devastation that had brought her to this place, Chornobyl was becoming more than a research trip. It was a crucible for ideas, a source of inspiration she hadn't expected to find amidst the decay and quiet recovery.

Genevieve leaned against the window, gazing out at the distant trees that bordered the dormitory, their bare branches etched against the twilight sky. The resilience of this land mirrored her own vision—not just to adapt, but to innovate, to create something enduring and meaningful from what others saw as ruin.

"It's all connected," she murmured. "The vineyard, the medicines, even the stars. Preservation isn't just about survival. It's about thriving in the face of challenge."

The thought energized her, sharpening her resolve. Tomorrow, she would dive deeper into her research, armed with not only the desire to understand but the determination to make a difference.

***

Ivan lingered in the background throughout the day as they were out on the field; a silent observer. His presence was a mix of professional duty and quiet curiosity. He seemed particularly intrigued by Marcel's experiments.

"What are you hoping to find, Dr. Dupont?" Ivan asked as Marcel adjusted the spectrometer.

"Patterns," Marcel replied. "Radiation disrupts, but it also creates. Somewhere in the disarray, there's a story—a story about origins. The same forces here shaped the universe billions of years ago."

"That's interesting that you talk of stories," Ivan said, his voice low and reflective. "This place has many stories to tell—a lot of havoc and many origins."
He leaned against a nearby tree, his weathered face catching the dim light filtering through the canopy. The lines around his eyes deepened as he gazed into the distance, as though seeing the past unfold before him.

"When I first came here, the silence was overwhelming. It's not the kind of quiet you find in nature or the peaceful countryside. It's an oppressive silence, full of echoes—of lives lost, of mistakes made, of resilience in the face of devastation. Every rusted swing set, every cracked pavement has a story."

Ivan paused, his scientific mind clearly processing the thoughts tumbling through his head. "Radiation is a curious force," he continued, turning to Marcel. "It's destructive, yes. But it's also transformative. Mutations, adaptations, changes we could never predict—it's all part of a larger cycle. Life doesn't just stop because of radiation. It shifts, and adjusts. The Red Forest is proof of that."

He gestured toward the horizon, where the stark, brittle trees of the forest loomed like sentinels. "Take the pine trees. Their needles turned red because of the high doses of radiation absorbed after the explosion. At first glance, it looked like death. But what's fascinating is how the ecosystem adapted. New species moved in, ones that could tolerate or even thrive in the conditions left behind. You see it in the insects, the plants, even the larger animals. It's as if nature took the disorder and turned it into something new—a different kind of balance."

Marcel listened intently, his analytical mind aligning with Ivan's observations. "It's like the universe," he said, his tone thoughtful. "Stars are born from the mayhem of collapsing gas clouds. Supernovae destroy, but they also create, scattering the elements needed for planets, for life. It's all connected."

Ivan nodded, his expression grave yet curious. "That's exactly it. Chaos isn't just destruction—it's also opportunity. Every mutation, every adaptation is a new branch in the story. And here, in this scarred land, we can observe those stories in ways we never could elsewhere. It's like a living laboratory, albeit a tragic one."

Genevieve, who had been listening quietly, finally spoke, her voice soft but resolute. "It's not just a story of survival," she said. "It's a story of persistence, of finding ways to thrive despite the odds. That's what we're here to learn, isn't it? How life—how nature—manages to endure, even in the face of devastation."

Ivan's eyes softened as he looked at her, a hint of admiration in his expression. "Yes. That's exactly it. And perhaps, in understanding how this place heals itself, we can learn how to better heal our own scars—on this planet, and beyond."

The three stood in silence for a moment, each lost in their own thoughts. For Ivan, it was a moment of reflection on the years he had spent studying the zone, watching as life crept back into the cracks of desolation. For Marcel and Genevieve, it was a reminder of the power of research—not just to understand but to transform. The story of Chornobyl, like the universe itself, was one of destruction giving birth to new beginnings.

Ivan nodded thoughtfully as he turned to Genevieve and asked "And you, Dr. Dupont?"

"Preservation," she said simply. "Nature has mastered it. I'm just trying to learn her secrets."

Ivan nodded, a faint smile tugging at the corner of his lips. "Ah, her secrets. This place has many secrets too. More than the rusting Ferris wheels and crumbling apartment blocks let on."

He leaned on his walking stick, his gaze drifting toward the desolate horizon. "Take the people who lived here before the disaster. Generations worked this land, cultivated it, celebrated harvests, and raised families. Then, in an instant, they were forced to leave everything behind. But some never did, or they found their way back. They're the 'Samosely'—the self-settlers."

Genevieve tilted her head, intrigued. "Self-settlers?"

"Yes," Ivan said, his voice tinged with reverence. "Mostly older people. They came back despite the warnings, despite the danger. They couldn't bear to be torn from their homes. They've adapted in ways that defy reason. They drink water from contaminated wells, eat produce grown in this soil, and yet some of them outlive people in the cities. No one can fully explain it. Maybe it's fortitude or tenacity; maybe it's something more."

Marcel raised an eyebrow, his scientific curiosity piqued.

"And what do they say about living here?"

"They talk about life, not death," Ivan said. "About their gardens, the seasons, and the animals that wander through. To them, this isn't a wasteland; it's home. And they've accepted its risks, its scars, in ways that almost seem poetic. Some even claim the land takes care of them, that there's a harmony here now that wasn't there before."

Genevieve glanced at Marcel, her expression thoughtful.

"It's almost as if they've preserved a way of life that the rest of the world has abandoned."

"Exactly," Ivan said, his eyes brightening. "It's not just the land that adjusts; it's the people, too. They're part of the ecosystem, adapting just like the animals and plants. It's another layer to the story here, one that speaks to the deeper connections we have with the places we call home."

He paused, then gestured around them. "Even the animals tell stories. Have you noticed? Wolves roam freely now, their numbers increasing. Wild boars dig up roots where children once played. And the birds—oh, the birds! Some species have vanished, but others have taken their place, thriving in the absence of human interference. It's as though life reclaims what we thought was lost."

Genevieve nodded, her mind racing with possibilities. "It's as if nature is rewriting itself, finding new ways to endure."

Ivan smiled at her. "Endurance, adaptation, reinvention—that's the language of this place. And if you listen closely, Dr. Dupont, perhaps you'll uncover the secrets you're looking for."

For a moment, they stood in silence, the air around them heavy with history and possibility. Each of them—Marcel, Genevieve, and Ivan—felt the weight of the zone's unspoken truths. And in that quiet, beneath the shadow of tragedy, they sensed a fortitude that could teach them all something profound.

Chapter 12

That evening, Ivan invited them to his quarters for dinner. The small dining area was warm, lit by a single lamp and a few candles. A modest meal of borscht, rye bread, and cured meats was laid out, accompanied by a bottle of Georgian wine. As they ate, the conversation turned personal.

"Did you two meet in a lab?" Ivan asked, pouring them another round of wine.

Genevieve chuckled. "In a lecture hall, actually. Marcel was giving a guest lecture on the formation of galaxies. I asked a question about entropy and how it shaped star formation."

"And I thought," Marcel interjected with a smirk, "who is this woman trying to dismantle my theory?"

Ivan laughed. "A match made in academia."

"Something like that," Genevieve said, smiling at Marcel. "But it wasn't just science. It was his passion for understanding the universe. He made the disarray of it all sound beautiful."

Marcel reached for her hand. "And you grounded me. You showed me that science isn't just about the cosmos—it's about what it means to be human."

For a moment, they sat in silence, the weight of their bond filling the room. Ivan raised his glass.

"To partnerships," he said, his voice earnest. "In science and life."

"To partnerships,"they responded raising their glasses.

Genevieve leaned back in her chair, savouring the final spoonful of the warm, earthy borscht. She set her spoon down and smiled at Ivan. "This is absolutely wonderful, Ivan. Did you make it yourself?"

Ivan chuckled, a hint of pride in his expression. "It's nothing fancy—just a simple recipe passed down from my mother. She believed a good bowl of borscht could cure anything."

"Well, she might have been right," Genevieve replied warmly. "I've always had a love for cooking and traditional dishes. There's something special about recipes that carry history, don't you think? At home, I spend hours in my herb and vegetable garden, experimenting with natural ingredients and blending flavours. It's my own little laboratory of sorts."

Ivan raised an eyebrow, intrigued. "A scientist in the kitchen as well? That's a talent I admire. What do you grow in this garden of yours?"

"Oh, everything from thyme and rosemary to heirloom tomatoes and Swiss chard," Genevieve said, her eyes lighting up. "It's such a joy to step outside and pick exactly what I need for a meal. And, of course, Marcel here always finds a way to pair our dishes with the perfect wine from the vineyard."

Marcel nodded, a satisfied smile on his face. "We've always had a passion for good food and dining. There's something about exploring the cuisine of a place that brings you closer to its soul. It's why we love to travel—tasting the dishes of the territory, and learning about the local ingredients and techniques. Every meal becomes a story, a memory."

Ivan poured himself another glass of wine, his demeanour softening. "I envy that, you know. The ability to travel, to experience the world through its flavours. Here, meals are more about survival than art. But even in simplicity, there's meaning. This borscht, for example—it's humble, but it carries the essence of this land."

Genevieve nodded thoughtfully. "Food does that, doesn't it? It connects people to their roots and to each other. Even the most modest meal can carry a wealth of tradition and emotion."

Ivan leaned back; his gaze distant. "You're right. And yet, I sometimes wonder if those connections are being lost. The world is moving so fast, leaving behind the slow rituals of cooking, of savouring. Maybe that's why I enjoy making this borscht—it reminds me to slow down, to appreciate what I have."

Marcel raised his glass. "To slowing down and savouring—both in meals and in life."

Genevieve and Ivan clinked their glasses with his, a shared moment of understanding passing between them. The dinner continued with lively conversation, their shared appreciation for food and its deeper meanings creating a bond that transcended their differences. In that modest dining room, amid the shadows of Chornobyl, the simple act of breaking bread became a celebration of tradition and human connection.

As they walked back to their quarters, the night was alive with the sound of crickets and the occasional rustle of leaves. Marcel paused, looking up at the clear sky, the stars scattered like diamonds on black velvet.

"Do you ever think about how small we are?" he asked, his voice soft.

Genevieve stood beside him, her gaze fixed on the same sky. "Small, but significant. Even the smallest elements shape the stars."

Marcel nodded, slipping his arm around her shoulders. "And here we are, trying to make sense of it all—on a scarred piece of Earth that's still finding its way back."

Genevieve leaned into him, her voice a whisper. "Resilience, Marcel. It's in everything—in the stars, in nature, and in us."

As they continued walking, the quiet of the night enveloped them, the weight of their shared purpose unspoken but deeply felt.

Chapter 13

The wind was eerily quiet on their third day as it wound through the skeletal remains of Pripyat. Once bustling with life, the abandoned city had surrendered to nature's relentless march. Crumbling buildings stood like tombstones, their empty windows staring out at a world that had moved on. Wildflowers and weeds grew defiantly through cracked asphalt, their bright colours in stark contrast to the grey desolation.

Marcel adjusted the settings on his Geiger counter; its soft clicks were the only sound besides their cautious footsteps.

"Radiation levels are still significant here," he muttered, his voice a low rumble that barely carried in the open air.

Genevieve, a few steps ahead, crouched to inspect a rusted swing set half-buried in grass. The equipment creaked faintly as the wind shifted. "Significant, yes," she replied, sealing a soil sample into a sterile container. "But not lethal—not anymore."

Marcel frowned. "Not immediately lethal. That's the problem with radiation—it lingers, subtle and unseen, until it's too late."

Genevieve stood, brushing her gloved hands together. Her face was partially obscured by the mask she wore, but her eyes gleamed with curiosity and something deeper—reverence. "And yet, life persists. Look around you, Marcel." She gestured to the stubborn greenery that had overrun the ruins, vines curling through shattered windows and birds nesting in collapsed roofs. "Nature is rewriting the rules. We should be studying this, learning from it."

"We are studying it," Marcel said, his tone sharper than he intended. He softened as he approached her, his gaze following hers to the vibrant flowers blooming around the playground. "But there's a difference between admiration and caution. This place—it's not natural. It's a scar."

Genevieve turned to him; her expression unreadable.

"Every scar tells a story. Isn't that what we do as scientists? Unravel those stories?"

The Geiger counter crackled louder as Marcel moved toward an overturned truck. The skeletal remains of its cab still bore the faded emblem of the Soviet Union. He ran his hand over the rusted metal, feeling the weight of history in its jagged edges. "Sometimes stories should be left untold."

Genevieve's laugh was soft, almost wistful. "And you call me the dreamer."

As they walked further into the exclusion zone, the silence seemed to press closer, heavy with the ghosts of the past. They reached what had once been a schoolyard, the faint outline of a hopscotch game still visible on the cracked concrete. Genevieve knelt again, carefully collecting samples of the moss creeping over the lines.

"You know," she said, her voice muffled by the mask, "there's a kind of poetry to it. This place—born of destruction, now nurturing life. It's almost... hopeful."

Marcel's jaw tightened. "Hopeful isn't the word I'd use." He scanned the area, the Geiger counter in his hand swinging back and forth like a divining rod. The clicks grew faster near the base of a crumbled wall, and he stopped, crouching to examine the soil. "What's hopeful about contamination? About death lingering for generations?"

Genevieve didn't answer immediately. She was watching a fox dart across the overgrown field, its fur a brilliant orange against the muted tones of decay and wondered whether it was the same fox she saw the other day. "Life doesn't need our permission to continue, Marcel. It just does."

For a moment, he envied her perspective. Where he saw danger and devastation, she saw resilience. It was part of what had drawn him to her all those years ago—her ability to find light in the darkest of places. But here, in Chornobyl, the stakes felt higher. He couldn't shake the feeling that they were meddling with something far beyond their understanding.

Genevieve's voice broke through his thoughts. "You're brooding again."

He glanced at her, his lips curving into a faint smile. "I'm thinking."

"Same thing," she teased. "You get that look when you're worried."

"Because I am worried, Genevieve." He straightened, his expression turning serious. "We're standing in the aftermath of humanity's hubris. A single mistake, a miscalculation—and this is the result. Entire lives erased. How can you look at this and feel anything but caution?"

She met his gaze, unflinching. "Because I see potential. I see what we can learn and how we can grow. You taught me that, Marcel. You taught me to ask questions and to challenge limits."

He sighed, running a hand through his hair. "And I also taught you to respect boundaries. This place—it's a reminder of what happens when we don't."

For a moment, they stood in silence, the weight of the conversation settling around them like the heavy air. Then Genevieve reached out, her hand brushing his. "I'll respect the boundaries, Marcel. But I won't stop asking questions."

Marcel studied her, the woman who had stood by his side through decades of triumphs and failures. He wanted to tell her to be careful, to stop pushing, to come back to the safety of their vineyard and leave this place behind. But he knew it was futile. Genevieve had always been fearless, and it was part of what he loved most about her.

"Just promise me one thing," he said finally.

"Anything."

"Don't let your curiosity blind you to the dangers."

Her eyes softened, and she nodded. "I promise."

The Geiger counter clicked steadily as they turned to leave, its sound fading into the distance as they walked away. But the seeds of tragedy could have already been sown, invisible and insidious, waiting to take root in the soil of their ambitions.

Chapter 14

The air was crisp as Marcel and Genevieve made their way back to the dormitory, the soft crunch of their boots against the snow breaking the evening's stillness. The desolate beauty of Chornobyl surrounded them, a haunting juxtaposition of silence and decay. Their earlier research session had left them both invigorated and contemplative, their findings stirring the embers of curiosity that had brought them here.

Genevieve clutched her notebook tightly, her breath visible in the cold as she glanced up at the darkening sky. "The way nature has adapted here—it's extraordinary," she said, her voice barely above a whisper. "Life always finds a way, doesn't it?"

Marcel nodded; his expression thoughtful. "Yes, but it's not without cost. The mutations we've seen in the samples tell a story of resilience, but also of struggle. There's a price to pay for survival in mayhem."

As they approached the dormitory, a figure emerged from the shadows near the entrance. His thick, fur-lined jacket and ushanka hat framed a weathered face that broke into a grin as they drew near.

"Ivan," Marcel greeted warmly, extending a gloved hand. "It's good to see you."

Ivan took Marcel's hand with a firm grip and nodded at Genevieve. "Good evening, my friends. How is your research progressing?" His thick Ukrainian accent lent a warmth to his words that contrasted with the icy surroundings.

Genevieve smiled. "It's been fascinating. Some of our findings are... unexpected. We're seeing patterns that might spark new lines of inquiry."
Marcel added, "The radiation here has affected everything in ways we're only beginning to understand. But it's not just the science—it's the stories this place holds. The way life continues, even after such devastation."

Ivan chuckled softly. "Ah, yes. Chornobyl has a way of captivating even the most seasoned scientists. It's a place that demands answers, though it rarely gives them freely."

Ivan moved to lean against the rusting frame of a nearby lamppost, his eyes narrowing as he looked off into the distance. "It's good that you're intrigued," he said, his tone shifting to something more sombre. "But let me ask you this: do you think you'll find answers that can solve the madness in the world?"

Genevieve tilted her head, curious. "What do you mean?"

Ivan sighed, pulling his jacket tighter around him. "The world seems to be unravelling, doesn't it? Wars in the east are escalating, and I hear the drug cartels are at war, too. It's causing mayhem in cities across the globe. People killing each other, crime rising—it feels like the world is crumbling under its own weight."

Marcel exchanged a glance with Genevieve. The thought was unsettling, but not entirely unfamiliar.

News of conflict and unrest had reached them even here, though it felt strangely distant in the quiet isolation of Chornobyl.

"I've heard similar reports," Marcel said cautiously. "But turmoil isn't new, Ivan. It's part of human history, just as it's part of the universe. What matters is how we respond to it."

Ivan laughed, a short, dry sound that echoed faintly in the cold. "True enough. But sometimes it feels like there are more questions than answers. Maybe I'm safe staying here in Chornobyl—away from all the madness."

He walked around as he explained then leaned against the dormitory's crumbling wall, the grey stone weathered and chipped like his face, which bore the marks of a life shaped by hardship and survival. Deep lines framed his eyes and mouth, each crease a testament to decades of experience, battles fought, and moments endured. His sharp grey eyes, though dulled slightly by fatigue, still carried a spark of wit, as if he refused to let the weight of the world extinguish his humour entirely.

He pulled a tattered scarf tighter around his neck, the fabric fraying at the edges but still offering some warmth against the biting wind. His hands, calloused and rough, gestured animatedly as he spoke, punctuating his words with a kind of resigned amusement.

"You know, Marcel," he said, waving vaguely toward the jagged skyline of Chornobyl's ruins, "maybe staying here isn't such a bad idea. At least here, the confusion feels… contained." He chuckled again, the sound more sardonic this time. "Out there? That's a whole other beast. At least the wolves here only howl. They don't sell drugs, start wars, or bring entire cities to their knees."

Marcel smiled, his breath misting in the frigid air. "You make it sound like you've found peace in all this decay, Ivan."

"Peace? No, my friend," Ivan said, shaking his head as he glanced at the ground. "It's not peace. It's…

manageable disorder. You can see the edges of it, predict its movements. Out there, in the cities? It's a storm with no eye. At least here, I know what I'm up against."

Genevieve, standing beside Marcel, studied Ivan thoughtfully. "You talk as if you've seen it all."

Ivan shrugged, one shoulder rising under his heavy coat. "Not all, but enough. Enough to know that the world is running faster and faster toward something it doesn't understand." He paused, his gaze distant for a moment before he pulled himself back to the present with a faint smile. "And enough to know that even in the middle of all this,"—he gestured broadly to the dilapidated buildings and the skeletal trees beyond—"there's beauty to be found."

Genevieve tilted her head, intrigued. "Beauty?"

Ivan nodded, his expression softening. "Yes. In the resilience of the land, the way nature reclaims what man tries to destroy. Even in the people who come here, like you two. Driven by curiosity, by a need to understand, to make sense of it all." He glanced at Marcel, his eyes narrowing with a teasing glint. "Though I'll admit, sometimes I wonder if scientists like you aren't just as chaotic as the world you're trying to study."

Marcel chuckled, accepting the playful jab. "Maybe. But chaos is the birthplace of understanding, isn't it?"

"Spoken like a true theorist," Ivan replied with a grin, though the weariness in his voice lingered. He straightened, adjusting his scarf again. "Still, I'm glad you're here. It's not every day we get visitors who see this place as more than just a graveyard of mistakes."

Genevieve smiled warmly. "It's not just mistakes we see. It's potential, too."

"That's the spirit," Ivan said, nodding approvingly. Then, his tone shifted, becoming more sombre. "Just don't let that potential blind you. This place has a way of reminding you of the cost of ambition."

For a moment, they stood in silence, the cold seeping into their bones. The distant sound of wind rustling through the trees filled the void. Ivan's rugged features softened slightly as he looked at the two of them, his usual guarded demeanour giving way to a flicker of genuine gratitude.

"You know," he said finally, his voice quieter, "it's good to see people who still care. About knowledge, about making things better. It gives an old man hope."

"You're hardly old, Ivan," Genevieve said, her tone light but sincere.

"Ah, flattery," Ivan said with a mock bow, his laugh more genuine this time. "Now you're trying to charm me. Careful, Genevieve, I might start to think you want something."

Marcel shook his head with a grin. "She's just being kind. Though, if you're offering a tour of the better mushroom patches around here, we wouldn't say no."

Ivan's laughter rang out, richer now, as he waved them off. "You'll have to earn that knowledge, my friend. But I'll tell you this—look where the trees are strongest. The mushrooms are always nearby."

With a final nod, Ivan stepped back toward the shadowed doorway of the dormitory. "Good luck with your research," he said, his voice carrying over the cold. "And remember—sometimes the answers aren't in the data. Sometimes they're in the questions you don't even know how to ask yet."

Marcel and Genevieve watched as he disappeared inside, the door creaking shut behind him. For a moment, they lingered in the cold, the weight of Ivan's words settling over them.

Suddenly the door reopened and Ivan reappeared. "And remember, please don't eat the mushrooms!" he said with slight concern.

Genevieve stepped closer to Ivan; her expression thoughtful. "The world does feel heavy with conflict right now, but perhaps it's not so different from what we see in nature. There's disruption, yes, but also resilience and adaptation. Maybe we can find ways to create balance."

Ivan regarded her with a wry smile. "Spoken like a true scientist. But tell me, Genevieve, does your work give you hope? Do you think the answers you're looking for can make a difference?"

She hesitated, glancing at Marcel. "I'd like to think so. The preservative I've been developing—it's designed to reduce waste, to extend the life of food and drink. It's a small thing, but small changes can ripple outward."

"And your work, Marcel?" Ivan asked. "You study the stars, the universe. What lessons do they hold for us here on Earth?"

Marcel's gaze drifted upward as if he could see beyond the clouded sky to the cosmos beyond. "The universe teaches us that mayhem is inevitable, but it's also necessary for creation. From the death of a star comes the birth of new elements, and new worlds. Maybe the confusion we see now is a precursor to something better—a chance for humanity to evolve."

Ivan nodded slowly; his expression unreadable. "Wise words, my friend. I hope you're right. But for now, I'll settle for a good night's sleep and a quiet day tomorrow. Good luck with your research. And remember— answers are never simple, but they're always worth seeking."

Marcel and Genevieve watched as Ivan disappeared into the night, his silhouette blending with the shadows. Marcel turned to his wife; his brow furrowed in thought.

"He's right," Marcel said softly. "The answers we're looking for won't come easily. But that doesn't mean we shouldn't try."

Genevieve placed a hand on his arm, her touch grounding. "We'll find them, Marcel. We'll find them."

As they entered the dormitory, the warmth of the interior enveloped them, a stark contrast to the biting cold outside.

But the questions Ivan had raised lingered, intertwining with their thoughts and, perhaps, their purpose.

Chapter 15

The following morning, the sun filtered through the mist, casting an ethereal glow on the forest where Marcel and Genevieve conducted their final collection. The air was crisp and carried the faint scent of damp earth and pine, mingled with the sweet tang of decaying leaves. A soft rustling of unseen creatures echoed through the trees, while the rhythmic crunch of their boots on the forest floor added a grounding rhythm to the serene stillness.

Genevieve slowed her pace; trailing her gloved fingers along the textured bark of a towering beech tree. The forest always had a way of centring her, its quiet resilience mirroring the intricacies of her work. Each patch of moss, each sprouting fungus, seemed to tell a story of survival and adaptation, a living testament to the persistence of life in even the harshest conditions. Her thoughts drifted to the mushrooms, their mycelial networks stretching unseen beneath the ground. They were nature's silent caretakers, breaking down the old to nourish the new.

She turned to Marcel, who walked a few paces ahead, his gaze fixed on the dense canopy above as if searching for patterns in the filtered sunlight. "You know," she said, her voice breaking the stillness, "mushrooms are remarkable creatures. They're like the universe's recyclers, taking what's decayed and turning it into something vital."

Marcel glanced over his shoulder, a wry smile playing at his lips. "Ah, yes, the philosopher of fungi speaks again. Tell me, are you planning to write an ode to mushrooms next?"

Genevieve laughed softly, shaking her head. "Don't mock them, Marcel. Without them, the entire ecosystem would collapse. Besides, they remind me that even in decay, there's renewal. Isn't that a bit like your stars? Dying supernovas creating the elements for new life?"

He stopped, turning to face her fully, his expression shifting to one of thoughtful amusement. "So, you're saying mushrooms are the black holes of the forest?"

"Precisely," she said with a grin, crouching to pick up a small piece of lichen-covered bark. "But they're more generous than black holes. They don't just consume; they give back."

Marcel chuckled, adjusting the strap of his field bag. "And here I thought I was the philosopher in the family. You're making me reconsider my lecture notes."

They walked on in companionable silence for a while, the interplay of light and shadow creating a kaleidoscope effect on the forest floor. Genevieve's thoughts returned to her research, the potential it held not just for revolutionising food preservation but for addressing larger issues of sustainability. It thrilled her to imagine a world where waste was minimised, and where resources were preserved with the same efficiency as the forest itself.

Ahead, a clearing revealed a patch of sunlight breaking through the mist, and Genevieve paused, scanning the undergrowth. The subtle rise of moss caught her attention, and she moved forward, her sharp eyes spotting a cluster of mushrooms nestled in the mossy undergrowth.

"These are fascinating," she murmured, carefully plucking one and turning it over in her gloved hand. "The way fungi thrive here, feeding on radiation—it's extraordinary."

"Please tell me you're not planning on making mushroom risotto?" joked Marcel.

Genevieve did not respond as she leaned closer to the tree to inspect the bark, her glove brushing its rough surface. A small, almost imperceptible particle of radioactive material clung to the synthetic fibres, unseen and unnoticed.

Nearby, Marcel packed his equipment into a case, pausing to glance at Genevieve. "Find something interesting?"

"Always," she replied with a soft smile, tucking the mushroom into a sample bag and wiping her gloved hands clean. "But it's nothing compared to what you uncover, Mr. Birth-of-the-Universe."

He chuckled, shaking his head. "It's all connected, Genevieve. The universe creates; nature adapts. Maybe that's the story we're chasing."

They stood for a moment in shared silence, the faint clicking of their Geiger counters the only sound.

***

That evening, Ivan hosted them for a final meal in his small dining room. The table was modestly set, but the atmosphere was warm. The meal began with *vareniki*—dumplings filled with potatoes and cheese—paired with a crisp Ukrainian vodka.

"I hope you've found what you came for," Ivan said, raising his glass.

"We have," Genevieve replied. "The adaptation of life here is remarkable. I've got a notebook full of ideas to take home for my work on food preservation. It's incredible how nature finds ways to survive."

Marcel nodded. "And I'm leaving with even more questions. The radiation here—it's like a glimpse into the forces that shaped the universe. I can't help but wonder what we're missing in our understanding."

Ivan smiled. "You scientists always looking for answers. That's what makes you different. And yet, you seem to find beauty in the unknown."
Genevieve glanced at Marcel, her eyes softening. "We do. And it's moments like this—conversations like this—that make it all worthwhile."

Ivan shuffled the steaming platter of *vareniki* on the table, the half-moon dumplings glistening with melted butter and garnished with a sprinkle of fresh dill. A small bowl of sour cream sat beside it, its creamy tang inviting.

"*Vareniki!*" Ivan announced with a hint of pride. "A humble dish, but one filled with tradition. My grandmother taught me to make these by hand when I was a boy. Every fold, every pinch—done with care. Inside, you'll find potatoes and caramelized onions. Simple, yet comforting."

Genevieve leaned forward, her eyes lighting up. "They look absolutely wonderful, Ivan. Food made with such care always tastes better. And isn't it true that the simplest dishes often carry the most meaning?"

Marcel smiled, pulling out a slender, dark bottle from his bag. "Ivan, your *vareniki* deserve a worthy pairing. This is one of our finest vintages—a special wine Jean-Pierre and I worked on together. I brought it along for a moment like this."

Ivan's eyes widened as Marcel set the bottle on the table, the label bearing the elegant crest of Château Dupont. "Your wine?"

"Yes," Marcel said, carefully uncorking the bottle. "This particular vintage is close to my heart. Jean-Pierre had the idea of experimenting with a new blend—one that marries tradition with a touch of innovation. We spent months perfecting it. The result is something we're both immensely proud of."

He poured a glass for Ivan, holding it up to the light to reveal its deep garnet hue. "This wine tells a story, just like your *vareniki*. It's a blend of the old and the new—much like our work at the vineyard. And much like the balance we see in nature here, constantly adapting and renewing itself."

Ivan took the glass, swirling it thoughtfully before taking a sip. He closed his eyes for a moment, savouring the rich, complex notes. "Magnificent," he said finally, his voice soft with appreciation. "You and your son—what a beautiful partnership. It's rare to see such passion passed down and shared."

Marcel nodded; his expression proud but humble. "It's more than work for us. It's a bond, a legacy. Every harvest, every bottle—it's a collaboration not just between us but with the land itself. Jean-Pierre has this remarkable way of respecting tradition while daring to innovate. It inspires me."

Ivan smiled warmly. "What you've built together—it's extraordinary. And it mirrors what I see in both of you as scientists. Your love for discovery, for understanding the world and its mysteries—it's something rare. You've brought that same love into your lives, into your family. Tonight, I realize I haven't just met brilliant minds. I've made dear friends."

He raised his glass. "And now, we can end this evening by sharing our food, our wine, and our friendship in science and research."

Genevieve lifted her glass, her eyes shining with sincerity. "Perhaps this friendship is more than that. It's a partnership—a meeting of kindred spirits."

The three clinked their glasses, a quiet but powerful acknowledgment of the bond they had formed. As they enjoyed the *vareniki* and sipped the wine, the room filled with warmth and laughter, a small but radiant light against the backdrop of Chornobyl's quiet shadows. In that moment, it wasn't just about food or wine or science—it was about connection, adaptability, and the beauty of shared purpose.

Before the meal ended, Genevieve said, "Ivan, you must come to Switzerland someday. We'll take you into the Alps, and you can pick mushrooms that are perfectly safe to eat. Marcel will even pair them with one of his wines."

Ivan laughed heartily. "I'll hold you to that. But I expect only the finest vintage."

***

The next morning, Ivan escorted them to the small station where the train back to Kyiv awaited. The platform was quiet, the morning chill sharp in the air.

"Thank you, Ivan," Marcel said, shaking his hand. "For your hospitality and your insights."

"You're always welcome here," Ivan replied.

Genevieve leaned in to give Ivan a light hug. "Don't forget your promise to visit us in Switzerland. And bring an appetite for cheese and wine."

As the train pulled away, Marcel and Genevieve waved to Ivan, his figure growing smaller against the backdrop of the forest.

Chapter 16

The journey back to Switzerland was long but pleasant. The landscapes shifted from the flat plains of Ukraine to the rolling hills of central Europe, eventually giving way to the rugged peaks of the Alps.

In their private train compartment, Marcel opened a bottle of wine they'd brought with them—a rich red from their family vineyard. Genevieve laid out a selection of cheeses, the aroma filling the small space.

"To Chornobyl," she said, raising her glass.

"To Chornobyl," Marcel echoed, clinking his glass against hers.

They sipped in silence for a moment, the rhythmic clatter of the train underscoring their thoughts.

"Do you remember our first trip to the Alps?" Genevieve asked, a playful smile on her lips.

"How could I forget?" Marcel said, laughing. "You got lost trying to identify mountain flowers, and I spent hours calling your name, thinking you'd fallen into a ravine."

"I was perfectly fine," she protested, laughing. "You're the one who panicked."

"I didn't panic," Marcel replied with mock indignation. "I was...concerned. Deeply concerned."

They both laughed, the kind of laughter born from years of shared adventures and love.
As the train wound through the mountains, they gazed out at the towering peaks dusted with snow, their wine glasses in hand.

"I love this place," Genevieve said softly.

"Me too," Marcel agreed, his voice tender. "It reminds me of why we do what we do. Nature, perseverance, life—it's all worth protecting."

The train ride felt like a journey between worlds. From the ashen desolation of Chornobyl, they returned to Switzerland's verdant embrace, where the vineyard's rows of vines whispered promises of renewal in the gentle breeze.

Genevieve leaned her head on his shoulder, and they sat in comfortable silence, the Alps standing sentinel as they journeyed home.

***

They both sat in the train reflecting on their trip as the rhythmic clatter of the train echoed softly in the quiet compartment, a soothing backdrop to the luscious green meadows at the foothills of the Alps rolling past the window.

Marcel leaned back in his seat, arms crossed, his gaze fixed on the horizon as though searching for answers in the gentle sway of the valleys. Genevieve sat opposite him, her notebook closed and resting on her lap. She studied her husband for a moment, noting the contemplative lines etched into his features.

"Are you satisfied, Marcel?" she asked softly. "Did you get what you came for?"

Marcel's eyes flickered toward her, a small smile tugging at the corner of his lips. "Satisfied?" he repeated, as though tasting the word. "Perhaps not in the conventional sense. But fulfilled? Yes, I think so. Chornobyl offered me something unexpected—a new way of seeing things. The disruption, the resilience of the land, the delicate dance between destruction and renewal. It reminded me that the universe operates in much the same way."

He shifted in his seat, his tone growing animated. "Think about it, Genevieve—radiation at Chornobyl is not unlike the radiation we observe in the cosmos. It's a force that both destroys and creates. Stars are born from the remnants of other stars, their death throes scattering the very elements that make up life itself. The patterns

I studied in the Exclusion Zone mirror the cycles of the universe. Perhaps this understanding can help us, paired with your research, refine not only our work in the winery but our grasp of the heavens."

Genevieve smiled; her green eyes alight with curiosity.

"You always manage to tie it back to the stars, don't you?"

Marcel chuckled, nodding. "I can't help it. The cosmos is where I learned to search for answers. But you—what about you, *mon amour*? Did Chornobyl give you what you were seeking?"

Genevieve's smile deepened, and she leaned forward, her voice brimming with quiet excitement. "More than I imagined. Watching how nature adapted in Chornobyl, how it fought to preserve itself against all odds—it gave me new ideas. I think I can redesign the preservation pills, not just to improve their function but to make them revolutionary. Imagine a preservative so efficient that it reduces waste entirely, not only in food but perhaps in medicine too. Sustainability, Marcel. It's not just about preserving what we have—it's about ensuring there's a future to preserve."

She paused, glancing out the window at the passing peaks, then back at him. "But above all that, I'm eager to go home, to take what we've learned and pour it into our work. I want to see the vineyards, feel the soil beneath my feet, and sit in the garden with Chantelle and Jean-Pierre. This trip—it's been extraordinary, but there's no place like the chateau."

Marcel reached across the table, taking her hand in his. "You're right. Home is where it all comes together. The research, the innovations—it all feels empty without the family to share it with."

They fell silent for a while, the train carrying them steadily toward their next chapter. Outside, the forest tapestry with peaks and rocks seemed to glow under the afternoon sun, their quiet beauty a reflection of the thoughts swirling in their minds.

Finally, Marcel spoke again, his voice tinged with affection. "Genevieve, do you think Jean-Pierre and

Chantelle will understand how much this trip meant to us?"

Genevieve squeezed his hand. "They'll feel it in the way we come back—not just with ideas but with renewed energy. And they'll see it in the way we embrace them, in the way we carry on the work together. That's what makes us a family, Marcel. We don't just share the work. We share the journey."

Marcel smiled, contentment settling over him. The train whistle blew, a gentle reminder that their return to the chateau—and to the heart of their lives—was drawing near.

Mario Zatta

Chapter 17

The evening air was crisp as Marcel and Genevieve Dupont stepped out of *La Belle Étoile*, their favourite Swiss bistro tucked away in the cobbled streets of Geneva. Marcel, ever the gentleman, held the door for his wife, who was bundled in a chic woollen coat. The couple's laughter over a shared memory about a university escapade softened as they stepped into the street, the ambiance pierced by flashing red and blue lights.

Marcel's smile faded. Police cars and ambulances were clustered at the far end of the street, their sirens silent now but their presence commanding. A small crowd of onlookers gathered behind yellow police tape, their murmurs floating on the night air. Marcel instinctively tightened his grip on Genevieve's arm.

"What could have happened here?" Genevieve asked, her voice tinged with concern.

Marcel's sharp eyes scanned the scene. "Nothing good, that's certain."

As they walked closer, they saw paramedics huddled over a prone figure lying on the pavement. Nearby, a police officer nudged another motionless figure with his boot, moving the limp arm to reveal a syringe still clutched in his hand. The faint trickle of liquid from a bottle of cheap alcohol spilt onto the stones, darkening the pavement beneath it.

Marcel's stomach churned. The stench of stale liquor and despair hung in the air, and the sight of vagrants sprawled across the scene filled him with a mix of pity and disgust.

"Another one," he muttered under his breath.

Genevieve pulled her coat tighter. "It's tragic, isn't it? To see lives unravel this way."

"Tragic? It's repugnant," Marcel replied, his tone biting. "This city prides itself on sophistication, yet we can't keep the streets free of this... filth. Drugs, alcohol, hopelessness—each one feeds the other."

Genevieve's gaze lingered on the paramedics lifting the body onto a stretcher, their motions heavy with the routine of seeing death too often. "They're still people, Marcel," she said softly. "Broken, yes, but human all the same."

Marcel didn't respond immediately. His focus had shifted to a detective speaking with another officer. Their hushed tones and serious expressions betrayed the gravity of the situation. He couldn't help but wonder what the full story was.

"Come, let's leave this place," Marcel said finally, steering Genevieve away. But as they walked back to their car, his mind churned with questions. Why had the vagrants succumbed so utterly? And why was the problem growing worse, even in a city as orderly as Geneva?

***

The morning sun streamed through the kitchen windows of the Dupont family chateau, casting a warm glow on the rustic stone walls and wooden beams. The scent of freshly brewed coffee filled the air, mingling with the subtle tang of ripe fruit from the bowl on the counter.

Genevieve, dressed in a tailored blouse and slacks, was preparing a delicate omelette at the stove, while Marcel read the day's paper, his expression stern. Jean-Pierre entered, his hair tousled, wearing a simple sweater and jeans. He moved to the fridge, poured himself a glass of orange juice, and switched on the television mounted on the far wall.

"Good morning, Jean," Genevieve said with a smile.

"Morning, *Maman*," he replied, taking a seat at the table.

As the TV screen flickered to life, a news bulletin blared: "Tensions escalate among cartel groups, with several reported shootings overnight in Geneva. Authorities fear a growing territorial war as rival factions clash over the lucrative drug trade."

Jean-Pierre froze mid-sip, his hazel eyes narrowing. "More violence. It's getting worse."

Genevieve turned off the stove, her look concerned as she listened to the report. The camera cut to an interview with the police commissioner, his tone grim. "We are seeing unprecedented levels of organised crime activity," he stated. "The gangs are not only fighting for territory but are now more brazen in their attacks. This is no longer a local issue—it's becoming a national crisis."

Marcel folded his newspaper with a sigh, placing it neatly on the table. "The city is unravelling," he remarked. "First, the addicts on the streets, and now this. It's all interconnected. Drugs fuel the crime, and the crime perpetuates the despair."

Jean-Pierre leaned back in his chair; his face thoughtful. "I wonder if it's more than that," he said. "The way these gangs are escalating—something feels different. It's like they're fighting over more than just drugs."

Genevieve joined them at the table, her gaze lingering on the screen. "It's heartbreaking to see this happening," she said. "And the police—how are they expected to contain such commotion?"

"They can't," Marcel replied bluntly. "Not with the current system. The root of the problem is the drugs, and as long as there's demand, there will always be supply."

Chantelle entered the room, her hair still damp from her morning shower. She wore a crisp blouse and skirt, her professional demeanour a sharp contrast to the relaxed atmosphere of the kitchen. "What's all this about?" she asked, pouring herself a cup of coffee.

Jean-Pierre pointed to the screen. "More gang violence. It's all over the news."

Chantelle frowned as she took a seat. "The hospital has been seeing a surge in cases tied to drug use. Overdoses, violence, infections... It's overwhelming."

Marcel looked at her thoughtfully. "It's a vicious cycle, one that society has been unable—or unwilling—to break."

The family sat in silence for a moment, the weight of the conversation settling over them. Outside, the vineyard stretched into the distance, a serene contrast to the turmoil unfolding in the city.

Chapter 18

After breakfast, Genevieve retreated to her laboratory—a bright, meticulously organized space adjacent to the chateau. Shelves lined with labelled jars and scientific equipment glinted under the fluorescent lights, reflecting her precision and passion for her work.

She donned a white lab coat and opened a drawer containing her personal protective equipment. With deliberate care, she slipped on her inner gloves. Staring at them, she remembered Chornobyl and recalled the heavy, thick ones she put on over them. The material, though thin, was a tangible reminder of the caution required when handling hazardous materials. Over these, she added latex gloves, snapping the edges around her wrists.

Her project was an ambitious one: developing a preservative pill for wine and spirits that would enhance shelf life while maintaining the integrity of the flavour. It was a challenge that combined her expertise in molecular chemistry with her deep appreciation for the family's winemaking legacy. She felt that current tablets on the market could be advanced in food and wine preservation.

Genevieve picked up a small vial containing a clear liquid, holding it to the light. The formula was nearly perfect, but she was determined to refine it further. She carefully measured the liquid into a beaker, her movements precise and practised.

As she worked, her mind wandered back to Chornobyl. The resilience of the environment there—the way nature adapted to radiation—had been both haunting and inspiring. She couldn't shake the memory of the mushrooms and wildflowers growing out of every crack.

Lost in thought, she adjusted the temperature on a small heating device and watched as the liquid in the beaker began to change colour. Her focus sharpened, and she jotted down notes in her journal.

Outside, the vineyard rustled in the gentle breeze as Genevieve walked to the window, her gloves in hand,

and gazed out at the vineyard. The golden light of the setting sun bathed the rows of vines, their shadows stretching long across the land. A sense of calm settled over her, but her thoughts lingered on the delicate balance she sought in her work.

As she stood there, her mind wandered to her younger self, a time when her ambitions had been as raw and unshaped as the early prototypes of her research. She could almost hear the bustling halls of the university, the hum of the laboratory equipment, and the soft rustle of notebook pages being turned.

She remembered one particular afternoon vividly. It was early autumn, and she and Marcel were sitting on the university lawn, their books spread out between them. He had been explaining the mechanics of star formation, his passion for the cosmos lighting up his face. She had teased him about "talking to molecules" even then, marvelling at his ability to find wonder in the smallest of particles and the vastness of space.

"You'll change the way we understand the universe someday," she had said, half-joking, as she propped her chin on her hand to watch him.

"And you," Marcel had replied, his voice warm and certain, "will change the way we survive it; nurture it, and preserve it."

Genevieve smiled at the memory. Back then, her focus had been on chemical compositions and reactions—how to extend the life of food and how to make resources last longer in extreme environments. She had dreamed of finding solutions to food scarcity and of ensuring that no child would go hungry in a world of abundance. Marcel had always believed in her, just as she had believed in him.

Her thoughts shifted to her children, to the moments when her roles as a scientist and mother intertwined. She had always encouraged Jean-Pierre to see the vineyard not just as a business but as a living, breathing ecosystem. She had inspired him to blend traditional methods with sustainable practices, ensuring the land would thrive for generations.

Her thoughts lingered on Jean-Pierre, her son who had grown into a man of quiet strength and conviction. She could picture him now, his hands expertly tending the vines, his hazel eyes scanning the rows of grapes with the precision of a scientist and the care of a farmer. Jean-Pierre had always possessed an innate connection to the land, but it was during one of their countless conversations in the vineyard that she had first seen the depth of his commitment.

"Nature gives us everything we need," he had told her, crouching to inspect a cluster of grapes. "We just have to respect her balance."

His words had stayed with her, echoing in moments like this when she questioned her own efforts. Jean-Pierre had taken her lessons about sustainable farming to heart, refusing to compromise the integrity of the vineyard for quicker yields or higher profits. Instead, he experimented with natural fertilizers, rotating crops to enrich the soil, and even planting wildflowers between the rows to attract pollinators.

Genevieve felt a swell of pride as she remembered the day Jean-Pierre had unveiled his idea for a completely organic vintage. He had brought her a bottle, his face alight with anticipation, and poured her a glass.

"Taste this, *Maman*," he had urged.

The wine had been unlike anything she had tasted before—vibrant, complex, and alive with the essence of the vineyard itself. It was as if Jean-Pierre had captured the spirit of the land in liquid form.

"It's beautiful," she had said, her voice thick with emotion.

Jean-Pierre had simply smiled, the kind of smile that reminded her so much of Marcel. "I want our wines to tell a story—not just about our family but about this land. If we can preserve its purity, its beauty, then we've done something meaningful."

That moment had cemented her resolve to push forward with her preservation research. She had always believed in the power of science to harmonise with nature, and

Jean-Pierre's passion reminded her why. Their mutual love for the environment and their shared belief in its resilience had created a bond that transcended the usual parent-child dynamic.

More than once, Jean-Pierre had been her sounding board, offering ideas that bridged their respective fields. When she had debated the best way to stabilise her preservative formula, it was Jean-Pierre who had suggested mimicking the fermentation process in wine to maintain balance without artificial additives.

And now, standing at the window, Genevieve smiled as she thought of her son. His dedication was more than just a professional ethos; it was a way of life. He treated the vineyard with the same care and reverence she gave her experiments. Together, they were proof that science and tradition could coexist, each enriching the other.

Jean-Pierre's vision for the vineyard wasn't just about producing excellent wine—it was about creating a legacy of respect for nature, one that would endure long after they were gone. And in her work, Genevieve saw the same goal reflected back at her: to preserve, protect, and honour the delicate balance of life.

With a deep breath, she returned her gaze to the vineyard, feeling a renewed sense of purpose. Her son's unwavering commitment had reminded her of the importance of her work—not just for their family but for the future they were all striving to protect.

She continued to reflect as a smile lit up her face. There vivid in her vision was Chantelle. Her brilliant, focused daughter, who had inherited her love for science. Genevieve had often marvelled at Chantelle's disciplined approach to medicine, knowing that her daughter's sharp intellect and compassionate heart would lead to extraordinary things.

She admired Chantelle's compassionate heart and the passion for healing that often left her in awe. Chantelle's work in the medical field had always inspired Genevieve to think beyond the confines of food preservation, pushing her to imagine the broader applications of her research. What if her discoveries could help extend the shelf life of critical medicines in remote areas? Or aid in preserving organs for transplant, saving countless lives? The possibilities Chantelle's work opened up were limitless and exhilarating.

Genevieve moved closer to the window and gazed out at the vineyard bathed in the warm light of the setting sun. Her lips curled into a gentle smile as she thought of Chantelle's quiet confidence, a trait she recognized as part of her own personality blended with Marcel's steady determination. Chantelle carried herself with grace, a calm assurance that seemed almost unshakable, yet her soft-spoken nature masked a strength and resilience that reminded Genevieve of herself in her younger days.

But there was something else, too. In Chantelle's piercing green eyes, Genevieve often saw the same thoughtful intensity that burned in Marcel's. It was a trait that made her daughter so effective as both a scientist and a healer, as she had an uncanny ability to observe the subtlest details and approach problems with measured precision.

Their bond had always been one of mutual admiration. Chantelle frequently expressed her respect for Genevieve's dedication to her work, telling her mother how much she admired her ability to balance scientific rigour with a love for life's simple joys. Genevieve, in turn, often found herself inspired by Chantelle's drive to make a difference in the world, her commitment to humanity, and her compassionate heart.

Chantelle's love for nature mirrored her mother's own, though it expressed itself differently. While Genevieve cultivated her garden and vineyards, Chantelle revelled in the harmony of the human body, seeing it as another of nature's masterpieces. It was this shared reverence for life that bound them together, creating a dynamic that was both inspiring and deeply personal.

Genevieve's thoughts drifted further, recalling the playful bond between Chantelle and Jean-Pierre. As children, they had been inseparable, running through the vineyard and laughing as they chased one another between the rows of vines. She could still hear their laughter echoing in her memory, and the image warmed her heart.

Even now, as adults, they retained that sibling connection. They loved to tease and challenge each other, often engaging in spirited debates that left everyone else smiling. Jean-Pierre would needle Chantelle about her meticulous habits, while Chantelle would mock his "romantic" attachment to the vines. But beneath the teasing was a profound respect and a shared belief in the value of hard work, honesty, and family.

Watching her children now—Chantelle with her steady, compassionate drive to heal and Jean-Pierre with his dedication to the vineyard—Genevieve felt an immense sense of pride. They had grown into remarkable people who carried forward the best of both their parents, yet each was uniquely themselves.

Standing at the window, as the last ray of light fell, Genevieve felt the full weight of her love for her family. The vineyard, the life they led, the bond they shared— it was all intertwined. She loved how Jean-Pierre's innovation blended with tradition to honour the land. She loved how Chantelle's compassion and intellect brought light into the world. She loved Marcel's unwavering curiosity and devotion, qualities that had drawn her to him all those years ago.

This was her legacy, she realized: not just the science or the wine but the family they had built together—a family rooted in love, respect, and a shared determination to create something lasting. With renewed energy, Genevieve turned back to her desk and tidied up, placing her gloves in the drawer. Whatever challenges lay ahead, she knew she was not alone. They were in this together, bound by their love for one another and their shared commitment to making the world just a little better.

The flashback warmed her, grounding her in the present. Her motivations for her work were no longer just about scientific ambition. They were about her family, their future, and the world they would leave behind.

Genevieve walked proudly to the kitchen, to the family that she loved so much. And as she walked, her resolve renewed, she whispered to herself, "For them—for all of us."

Chapter 19

The first rays of sunlight filtered through the large, east-facing windows of the Dupont family kitchen. The room, warmed by the aroma of freshly brewed coffee and the comforting scent of toasted oats, was a haven of calm before the day's bustle. Genevieve stood at the counter, her hands deftly arranging bowls of roasted muesli, sliced fruit, and creamy yoghurt. A pot of coffee percolated nearby, its rich aroma mingling with the faintly sweet scent of honey she drizzled over the muesli.

Chantelle was already seated at the long wooden table, cradling a steaming cup of coffee between her hands. Her hair was loosely tied back, and shadows under her green eyes betrayed the exhaustion she couldn't quite shake. Her scrubs, still faintly creased from last night's shift, hinted that she had barely had time to change before collapsing into bed hours earlier.

Jean-Pierre breezed in, his hair slightly dishevelled and his steps buoyant with the energy of someone ready to tackle the day. He froze mid-step, assessing his sister with a teasing smirk. "What's wrong, sis?" he asked, leaning casually against the counter. "Had a long night again?"

Chantelle groaned, leaning back in her chair. "Another never-ending night at the hospital. Cases just kept pouring in. I barely sat down." She sipped her coffee and added, "And don't even get me started on some of the gang-related injuries. It feels like the violence out there is only getting worse."

Jean-Pierre pulled up a chair across from her and began helping himself to muesli. "Sounds rough. You know, you should spend a day in the vineyard. Guaranteed therapy. Nothing like fresh air, sunlight, and a little hard work to reset the mind."
Chantelle rolled her eyes. "You mean a day of being bossed around by you?"

"Supervised," he corrected with a grin. "It's called quality time, Chantelle. You should try it."

Genevieve smiled from the counter as she refilled Chantelle's mug. "Jean-Pierre might have a point. Fresh air can do wonders."

***

As the siblings bantered, the muted sound of the television in the corner went unnoticed. A news anchor's voice droned on, the words barely cutting through the familial chatter. The screen showed a stern-faced police chief giving a statement:

"Gang-related violence has escalated sharply in the past week. Authorities are working tirelessly to curb the spread, but the situation remains volatile. We urge citizens to remain vigilant..."

Genevieve turned off the stove and carried a fresh pot of coffee to the table. "Come now, breakfast is getting cold. You two can argue about work-life balance later."

Jean-Pierre turned his attention back to his meal, grinning. "Fine, but only if Chantelle agrees to a day off."

"Not today," Chantelle replied. "Some of us have real jobs."

"Unlike winemaking?" Jean-Pierre feigned offence, dramatically clutching his chest. "You wound me, doctor."

Genevieve laughed softly, patting her son's shoulder as she sat down. "You two could debate for hours. Let's just enjoy breakfast."

Moments later, Marcel strolled into the kitchen. He was impeccably dressed, as always, in a crisp white shirt and tailored trousers, his silver hair neatly combed. His sharp gaze softened as he took in the cosy scene before him.

"Good morning, family," he said, his voice carrying a warmth that belied his typically reserved demeanour.

"*Papa*," Jean-Pierre greeted, his tone teasing. "We were just discussing Chantelle's terrible taste in leisure activities."

"Don't drag me into your battles," Marcel said with a small smirk, pouring himself a cup of coffee. He took a moment to inhale its aroma before addressing Genevieve. "Today is a beautiful day for the mountains. Shall we go hunting for mushrooms, *ma chérie*?"

Genevieve's eyes lit up, her smile breaking through the calm efficiency she always exuded. "Oh, Marcel, that sounds wonderful. It's been far too long since we've gone."

"You're really going mushroom hunting?" Jean-Pierre interjected with mock incredulity. "What century is this?"

"Leave them alone," Chantelle said, grinning despite her tiredness. "It's sweet. And besides, they'll be out of the way, which means we don't have to supervise them."

Genevieve raised an eyebrow at her children. "You behave yourselves, or no mushrooms for dinner."

Chantelle and Jean-Pierre laughed as Marcel offered Genevieve his arm. "Come, my love," he said. "The forest awaits."

Chapter 20

The alpine forest stretched out before Marcel and Genevieve like a scene from a fairy tale. Tall pines swayed gently in the breeze, their needles creating a soft carpet underfoot. Sunlight filtered through the canopy, casting golden-dappled light on the forest floor. The crisp, earthy scent of the woods invigorated their senses.

Genevieve moved ahead with a basket in hand, her eyes scanning the ground for telltale signs of chanterelles and porcini. Marcel followed, his hands tucked into the pockets of his jacket, his gaze occasionally drifting upward to admire the towering trees.

"You always find the best spots," Genevieve said, pausing to examine a cluster of mushrooms near a mossy log. "I don't know how you do it."

"Years of observation," Marcel replied with a slight smile. "It's all about understanding the patterns of nature, my dear."

Genevieve carefully harvested the mushrooms, placing them into her basket. "You make it sound so scientific."

"Everything is," Marcel said, his tone thoughtful. "Even something as simple as mushroom hunting. It's all a matter of paying attention to the variables."

Genevieve laughed softly. "Ever the scientist."

The forest was alive with muted sounds: the rustling of leaves overhead, the soft crunch of earth beneath their boots, and the occasional trill of a bird cutting through the cool air. Genevieve moved with a practised ease, her sharp eyes scanning the mossy undergrowth. Marcel followed a short distance behind, pausing every now and then to inspect the ground with curiosity.

"Genevieve," he called out, crouching beside a cluster of mushrooms. "What about this one? It doesn't look like anything I've seen before."

She turned, adjusting her basket and stepping closer.

Marcel pointed at a small, pale mushroom with a delicate cap and a slender stem.

"Is it poisonous?" he asked, his brow furrowed in mock seriousness.

Genevieve knelt beside him, her fingers gently brushing the mushroom's surface. "See here?" she said, pointing to the gills underneath the cap. "They're pale and closely spaced. That, along with the smooth cap and absence of a ring, suggests it's likely edible. But—" she glanced up at him with a teasing smile—"we don't take chances unless we're absolutely sure. A wrong bite could be your last."

Marcel chuckled, leaning back on his heels. "You know, the mushrooms we saw in Chornobyl didn't have these features you described, and they were most definitely poisonous. Mutated, even."

Genevieve shot him a playful glare. "Behave yourself, Marcel. Otherwise, you won't be getting any of my mushroom risotto tonight."

Marcel put a hand to his chest, feigning shock. "Not your risotto? Now that's a real tragedy."

She laughed, shaking her head as she stood. "Keep teasing, and I might just let you forage for your own dinner."

He grinned, rising to his feet and brushing dirt off his hands. "I wouldn't dare. Your risotto is worth its weight in gold. I'll be on my best behaviour."

Genevieve gave him a knowing look before returning to her search, the playful moment lingering between them like a shared secret. Marcel lingered for a moment, gazing at the mushroom again, then at Genevieve as she moved gracefully through the trees.

"Nature's resilience," he murmured to himself, smiling.

"And yours, too, mon amour."

***

As they walked deeper into the forest, their conversation turned to their respective projects. Genevieve spoke animatedly about her preservation techniques, her words tinged with pride and excitement.

"I have an interested buyer for my new preservative formula," she said, her eyes shining. "It's a major company, Marcel. If this goes through, we could revolutionize food and wine preservation. Imagine—products that last longer without compromising quality. It could change the industry."

Marcel listened intently, nodding as she spoke. "It's remarkable, Genevieve. You've taken an idea and turned it into something tangible, something impactful."

She stopped walking and turned to face him. "You really think so?"

"I do," he said, his tone earnest. "But more than that, I think you're doing this for the right reasons. It's not just about innovation; it's about leaving the world better than we found it."

Genevieve smiled, her heart swelling at his words. "That means a lot, Marcel. Truly."

"And what's the next step?" he asked.

"Well, there's a meeting with the buyer next week," she said, her voice steady despite the flicker of nerves in her eyes. "If all goes well, we could finalize the deal within a month."

Marcel placed a reassuring hand on her shoulder. "It will go well. You've prepared for this."

***

They continued their walk, their conversation shifting to their shared love of nature. Genevieve marvelled at the perseverance of the forest and how it thrived despite the challenges it faced.

"It's fascinating," she said, running her fingers over the bark of a tree. "Nature always finds a way to adapt. It's a lesson we could all learn from. Remember Chornobyl Marcel."

Marcel nodded; his gaze distant. "There's a certain poetry to it, isn't there? The cycles of destruction and renewal. It's what drew me to study supernovas. They're the ultimate example of nature's paradox— unimaginable destruction giving birth to new stars and worlds."

Genevieve smiled. "And here we are, studying mushrooms and stars, each in our own way."

"Both equally important," Marcel said with a small grin. "After all, where would we be without mushroom risotto?"

Genevieve laughed, the sound echoing through the quiet forest. It was a moment of lightness, a reminder of the joy they found in each other's company, even amid life's challenges.

As the sun began to dip lower in the sky, Marcel and Genevieve made their way back to the chateau, their basket brimming with mushrooms. The forest, now bathed in the warm hues of late afternoon, seemed to bid them farewell.

"I think this has been one of our more successful outings," Genevieve said, glancing at the basket.

"Success is subjective," Marcel replied. "But yes, I agree."

They walked in companionable silence for a while before Genevieve spoke again. "Thank you, Marcel. For today."

"For the mushrooms?" he teased.

"For the support," she said, her voice soft. "It means more than I can say."

Marcel smiled, his hand brushing hers as they walked. "Always, my love. Always."

Chapter 21

The late afternoon sun bathed the Dupont estate in golden light, illuminating rows of perfectly cultivated vines stretching into the horizon. Genevieve Dupont stood in the office overlooking the vineyard, her hands lightly clasped in front of her. She had always found solace in the view—the symmetry of the rows, the promise of the land, and the reminder of her family's legacy.

Today, however, her mind was consumed by the meeting ahead. A licensing deal for the winery's groundbreaking preservative was on the table, a deal that could secure Chateau Dupont's future for generations.

The soft knock on the door pulled her from her thoughts.

"Madame," came Marie's voice, "your guest has arrived."

Genevieve smoothed her blouse and straightened her posture. "Thank you, Marie. Please escort him to the study."

A few moments later, Genevieve stepped into the study to find Giovanni Russo waiting. His presence was commanding, his tailored suit and easy confidence marking him as a man accustomed to getting what he wanted.

"Dr. Dupont," he greeted warmly, extending a hand. "Thank you for seeing me."

Genevieve offered a polite smile as they shook hands. "Mr. Russo, welcome. I trust your journey was pleasant?"

"Very," he replied, his dark eyes scanning the room. "Your estate is exquisite. Truly a gem in the heart of Switzerland."

"Thank you. Shall we get down to business?" She gestured toward the armchairs by the fireplace, her tone calm but efficient.

As they settled in, Giovanni opened his briefcase, producing a series of documents. "Your preservative has caught the attention of some very influential players in the global wine industry," he began. "Its ability to extend the shelf life of wine without compromising quality is nothing short of revolutionary. I'm here to propose a partnership—exclusive licensing rights that will take your product to an international stage."

Genevieve listened attentively; her expression thoughtful.

"Mr. Russo, I appreciate your interest. But exclusivity is a significant commitment. Our preservative is the result of years of careful research and testing. It's not just a product; it's a reflection of our values as winemakers."

Giovanni's smile didn't falter, but his eyes sharpened.

"And I respect that. But with my resources, we could bring this innovation to markets you'd never reach on your own. Think of the possibilities—your family's name could become synonymous with excellence worldwide."

The discussion continued, a careful back-and-forth as Genevieve held her ground. She was resolute in protecting the integrity of her family's creation, insisting on strict oversight of its use.

Finally, after nearly an hour, they reached an agreement. Giovanni secured a limited licensing deal that would allow him to introduce the preservative to select markets, while Genevieve retained full control over its production and distribution.

As they signed the papers, the firelight flickered in the room, casting shadows that seemed to dance with the tension.

After Giovanni departed, Genevieve returned to the office. She felt a sense of accomplishment, though it was tempered by exhaustion. She poured herself a glass of wine, her gaze drifting once more to the vineyard beyond the window.

Her thoughts turned briefly to the early days of developing the preservative. The process had been fraught with challenges, many of which she had overcome through sheer determination. Some aspects of the research—such as the unexpected stability provided by a rare mineral sourced from her trips to Eastern Europe—still puzzled her.

She remembered her visit to a facility near Chornobyl, where she had worked with specialists studying the region's unique soil composition. The samples she'd brought back had been promising in furthering her research and enhancing the preservative's effectiveness.

Just as Marcel stated, she thought to herself. Through confusion and disruption comes birth.

Chapter 22

The fluorescent lights of the hospital hallway cast a sterile, clinical glow, but to Chantelle Dupont, the scene before her was anything but ordinary. She stood at the nurse's station, reviewing a chart her face concentrated, her green eyes scanning for patterns that didn't add up.

The cases had started trickling in weeks ago—overdoses that weren't quite overdoses, erratic heart rates with no clear cause, and, most unsettling of all, patients who simply didn't survive despite their symptoms being initially mild.

"Dr. Dupont?" a nurse called, snapping her from her thoughts.

"Yes?" Chantelle responded, setting the chart aside. "It's Room 304—the new patient brought in an hour ago. Unresponsive. The paramedics mentioned drug use, but the tox screen came back inconclusive."

Chantelle nodded, her heart sinking as she headed toward the room. This had become all too common: patients presenting with signs of drug use, yet toxicology tests showed no trace of the usual culprits. She pushed the door open and found a man in his early 30s lying still on the hospital bed, his skin pale and clammy.

"What's his story?" she asked the attending nurse, who was adjusting the IV drip.

"Found unconscious in an alley. No visible needle marks, but he had a bottle of alcohol in his hand and some pills in his pocket. He coded once during transport, but they got him back."

Chantelle examined the patient, her hands steady despite the unease growing within her. His pupils were constricted, and his breathing was shallow but rhythmic. She ordered another round of tests, though she suspected the results would be the same: inconclusive.

After checking his vitals, she stepped out of the room, pulling off her gloves. The nurse followed her expression mirroring Chantelle's concern.

"It's strange, isn't it?" the nurse said. "We've been seeing more of these cases lately. Not overdoses, not infections, just... unexplained failures."

"Yes," Chantelle admitted, her voice low. "It's like the body just gives up, and we don't know why."

The two parted ways, and Chantelle headed to the break room, needing a moment to process. She sat by the window, staring out at the city skyline as her mind replayed the events of the past month. Each case was like a puzzle with pieces that didn't fit—except, disturbingly, they all had one thing in common: a combination of drug use and alcohol.

Her thoughts drifted to the discussion at breakfast that morning. The news of gang violence and rising tensions in the city mirrored the bedlam she was witnessing in the hospital. Was there a connection? The question nagged at her, but she didn't yet have enough evidence to draw conclusions.

Her phone buzzed, pulling her from her reverie. It was a text from her colleague, Dr. Bernard, who worked in the toxicology lab.

Bernard: *The latest samples are negative for common substances. Want to brainstorm later?*

Chantelle typed a quick reply: *Absolutely. Something's not adding up.*

Chapter 23

The Dupont family gathered in the living room that evening, the fireplace casting a warm glow against the stone walls. Marcel sat in his usual armchair, a glass of red wine in hand, while Genevieve worked on her laptop at the corner desk. Jean-Pierre leaned against the mantel, his arms crossed, and Chantelle occupied the loveseat, a medical journal open on her lap.

The television played softly in the background, tuned to the evening news. But as the anchor's voice grew urgent, Jean-Pierre grabbed the remote and increased the volume.

"Reports continue to pour in regarding a sudden surge in unexplained deaths among drug users," the anchor announced, her expression grim. "Authorities are scrambling to identify the cause, but early indications suggest that alcohol may also play a role. Experts are calling this a potential public health crisis."

The screen cut to footage of paramedics loading a stretcher into an ambulance, followed by an interview with a prominent toxicologist.

"These cases defy conventional explanation," the expert said, shaking his head. "We're seeing individuals with low levels of common recreational drugs and moderate alcohol consumption, yet the outcomes are catastrophic. It's as if their bodies are reacting to a hidden toxin we've never encountered before."

Genevieve paused her typing, her face lined with concern as she glanced at the screen. Marcel's grip on his wine glass tightened, his analytical mind already racing.

"This is escalating," he said, his tone heavy.

Jean-Pierre's expression darkened as he leaned forward, the familiar warmth in his eyes replaced by worry. "What do they mean alcohol is involved?" he asked, his voice sharp. "How? If this becomes a public health concern, it's going to devastate the liquor industry. Vineyards like ours will be hit the hardest."

Chantelle, looking up from her journal, regarded her brother thoughtfully. "Jean-Pierre, it's not just about the industry. People are dying. What I've seen at the hospital is terrifying—cases that don't make sense, patients whose bodies just give out for no apparent reason. And now we're hearing alcohol might be involved. This is bigger than our vineyard."

"I know it's bigger," Jean-Pierre countered, his tone defensive. "But think about what happens next. If authorities start linking alcohol to these deaths, they'll come after producers first. It won't matter whether our wine is the problem or not—our reputation could be ruined by association."

Marcel raised a hand, his voice calm but firm. "Let's not jump to conclusions. The media is speculating, and so are the scientists. Until there's definitive evidence, we can't assume anything."

Jean-Pierre sighed, rubbing the back of his neck. "I just don't want to see everything we've worked for destroyed because of something beyond our control."

The screen shifted to a press conference with the head of the World Health Organization. The official's expression was grave as she addressed the reporters.

"This phenomenon is not isolated to one region," she said. "Similar cases are being reported across Europe and in parts of North America. Our laboratories are working tirelessly to identify the cause, but we urge the public to exercise caution. Avoid combining alcohol with any recreational substances until we have more answers."

The room fell silent as the family absorbed the magnitude of the crisis. Outside, the vineyard stood in tranquil contrast to the commotion being described on the screen.

"It's like a ticking time bomb," Jean-Pierre said finally. "And no one knows when or where it'll go off next."

Chantelle closed her journal, her mind racing. "I need to reach out to my colleagues," she said. "If we can compare notes, maybe we'll find a clue."

Marcel nodded; his expression steely. "And I'll make some calls of my own. If this is as serious as it seems, it may require a scientific perspective beyond what the authorities can offer."

Genevieve turned back to her laptop, her fingers hovering over the keyboard. She hesitated for a moment, then resumed typing.

As the news broadcast continued, the Duponts exchanged uneasy glances. For Marcel and Chantelle, the storm brewing was a mystery to solve. For Jean-Pierre, it was a threat to the legacy they had worked so hard to build.

Chapter 24

The dining room in the Dupont chateau was a masterpiece of old-world charm and modern elegance. The long oak table, polished to a gleaming shine, was laden with platters of roasted vegetables, fresh bread, and a selection of wines from the family's vineyard. The chandelier above cast a warm glow, adding an intimate atmosphere to the gathering.

Genevieve sat at one end of the table; her posture graceful as she poured a glass of chardonnay for herself. Marcel, at the opposite end, swirled his wine thoughtfully, his face frozen as if lost in contemplation. Chantelle and Jean-Pierre occupied the middle seats, their plates half-filled as the conversation ebbed and flowed.

"So," Genevieve said, her voice soft but inquisitive, "how was work today, Chantelle? You've been very quiet."

Chantelle, dressed in her usual understated elegance, set her fork down and leaned back slightly, her deep green eyes reflecting a hint of unease. "It's been… unsettling," she admitted, her voice low.

Jean-Pierre, who had been buttering a slice of bread, paused mid-motion and looked up. "Unsettling how?" he asked.

"I've been seeing patients with symptoms that don't add up," Chantelle explained. She rested her elbows on the table and clasped her hands as if trying to find the right words. "There's this pattern—young people, seemingly healthy, but they're collapsing. Some come in comatose, others with seizures or heart failure. The drug levels in their systems are low, sometimes barely detectable. It doesn't make sense."

Marcel's expression sharpened; his scientist's mind instantly engaged. "And these are all drug users?"

Chantelle nodded. "Yes, but it's not consistent. Some had alcohol in their systems too, but not in quantities that should cause this kind of reaction. It's as if their bodies are shutting down for no apparent reason."

Jean-Pierre frowned, his protective instincts kicking in. "Are you safe treating them? If it's something contagious—"

"It's not contagious," Chantelle interrupted, though she appreciated his concern. "At least, there's no indication of that. But it's frightening. We had a patient last night—a young woman, barely twenty-two. She was at a party, had a couple of drinks and, according to her friends, took half a tablet of MDMA. She collapsed within minutes. By the time she got to the hospital…" Chantelle's voice trailed off, and she shook her head.

"She didn't make it," Genevieve said softly, her expression sympathetic.

Chantelle confirmed with a nod. "Her tox screen was clean apart from the MDMA and a small amount of wine. But there was something about her case… It felt different like her body reacted to something we couldn't see or measure."

Marcel leaned forward, his elbows resting on the table. "You said it felt different. How so?"

Chantelle hesitated, organizing her thoughts. "There's a certain pattern to overdoses—whether it's opioids, amphetamines, or alcohol poisoning. But these cases are different. The symptoms don't match what we'd expect from any known substance. It's almost as if the drugs and alcohol are acting as catalysts for something else entirely."

Marcel's mind churned, drawing on decades of scientific knowledge. "Could it be a new substance? Something undetectable with current toxicology tests?" "That's what we're starting to suspect," Chantelle replied. "But if that's the case, it's spreading fast. And it's terrifying to think how many more could be affected."

Jean-Pierre, his jaw tight, set his bread down untouched. "If this starts affecting alcohol consumption, the industry could be in serious trouble. People will panic, boycott products, and start pointing fingers. And vineyards like ours—and all the small, family-run operations out there—will be the first to suffer."

"This isn't about the vineyard," Chantelle said again, a rare edge in her voice. "This is about lives. People are dying, Jean-Pierre. It's not just numbers on a balance sheet."

Marcel intervened; his tone measured but firm. "Jean-Pierre isn't wrong to consider the potential fallout, Chantelle. But for now, our priority is understanding what's happening. If this phenomenon spreads, it could have far-reaching consequences—for society, for public health, and yes, even for the economy."

The table fell silent for a moment, the gravity of the discussion sinking in.

Genevieve broke the tension by pouring more wine into Marcel's glass. "Whatever this is," she said softly, "We stick together and we support each other as a family."

Chantelle offered a small smile of gratitude, though her unease lingered. The conversation shifted to lighter topics, but the undercurrent of tension remained, like a storm brewing just beyond the horizon.

* * *

The television in the Dupont living room flickered to life, filling the space with the steady hum of news broadcasts. Marcel and Genevieve sat on the couch, while Jean-Pierre stood near the window, arms crossed as he gazed out at the vineyard. Chantelle, perched on the armrest of a chair, watched the screen intently.

"Breaking news," the anchor announced, her tone grave. "Authorities across Europe and North America are grappling with a surge in unexplained deaths among teenagers to elder adults. Early reports suggest a troubling link between these fatalities and the use of drugs in combination with alcohol."

The screen displayed a montage of chaotic scenes: ambulances racing through city streets, forensic teams examining dimly lit party venues, grieving families clutching photographs of lost loved ones.

"In cities from Paris to Los Angeles," the anchor continued, "local governments are reporting a significant decline in crime rates, particularly in areas plagued by drug-related violence. While this may seem like a silver lining, experts warn that the underlying cause of these deaths remains a pressing mystery." Jean-Pierre turned from the window; his expression dark.

"Declining crime rates," he muttered. "That's one way to spin it."

"It's a grim trade-off," Chantelle said, her voice low. "Fewer dealers on the streets because they're dying too."

The broadcast shifted to an interview with a criminologist. "We're witnessing a collapse of the illicit drug trade," the expert said. "With users and distributors alike succumbing to this unknown phenomenon, the power dynamics among cartels are shifting. Rival factions are vying for control, leading to increased violence in some areas."

Jean-Pierre sighed, running a hand through his hair. "So now we have a health crisis and a brewing gang war. Wonderful."

Genevieve placed a comforting hand on his arm. "This isn't just about us, Jean-Pierre. The entire world is grappling with this."

The next segment featured a harried-looking government official addressing reporters. "We urge the public to avoid using recreational drugs and to consume alcohol responsibly," he said. "Our laboratories are working tirelessly to identify the cause of these tragic deaths. In the meantime, we must remain vigilant."

Marcel rubbed his chin thoughtfully. "If they're calling for restraint, it means they suspect a connection but can't prove it yet."

"Which only fuels speculation," Chantelle added. "People are already panicking. Patients are coming to the hospital just because they had a drink and feel a little off. The psychological impact alone is overwhelming."

As the broadcast continued, the family exchanged uneasy glances. The crisis was no longer an abstract problem; it was unfolding in real-time, its ripple effects reaching every corner of their lives.

***

The soft glow of the evening sun spilled through the windows of the chateau, casting long shadows across the living room as the Dupont family lingered after the news bulletin. Though the room was quiet, the weight of the crisis hung heavily in the air, unspoken but present.

Jean-Pierre sat apart, staring into the fireplace as if the flickering flames held the answers to the storm of thoughts in his mind. His earlier words echoed back to him with an unsettling clarity:

"If this starts affecting alcohol consumption, the industry could be in serious trouble. People will panic, boycott products, and start pointing fingers. And vineyards like ours—will be the first to suffer."

The truth of that statement gnawed at him. His life, his work, his future—it all revolved around the vineyard. Every vine, every cluster of grapes, every bottle of wine bore the imprint of his labour and dedication. He had poured his heart into the land, preserving the traditions handed down by his grandfather, while also championing sustainability and innovation to ensure the vineyard's resilience for generations to come.

Jean-Pierre's thoughts turned to his mother. Genevieve had been more than a guide in his efforts to modernise and refine their practices. She had been his anchor. Her deep scientific knowledge had brought unparalleled advancements to their winemaking processes, but her influence extended far beyond technical expertise. Her quiet encouragement; her belief in his "fantastic ideas," as she called them, had bolstered him on days when the work seemed too daunting, the challenges insurmountable.

More than a scientist, she had been a mother—loving, supportive, and unwavering in her faith in him. Jean-Pierre smiled faintly, remembering how she would join him in the vineyard, her sleeves rolled up, her hands delicately tending to the vines as she spoke about balance, harmony, and the importance of nurturing not just the grapes, but the soil, the ecosystem, and the family who worked alongside it.

And then there was his father. Marcel's presence in the vineyard and winery was a constant reminder of the values Jean-Pierre held dear: discipline, innovation, and tradition. Marcel brought his precision as a scientist into every aspect of winemaking, blending it seamlessly with a deep respect for the craft.

Jean-Pierre cherished their camaraderie. His father's stories about his father—the family patriarch who had planted most of the vines—fuelled Jean-Pierre's sense of responsibility and pride. Those stories were woven into the fabric of their family, just like the roots of the vineyard that bound them together.

His chest tightened as he thought about what was at stake. This land, this legacy—it wasn't just a business. It was their history, their identity, their home. He thought back to his childhood when the vineyard had been his playground. He and Chantelle had spent countless days racing through the rows of vines, their laughter mingling with the rustling leaves. The vineyard wasn't just a place where grapes grew; it was where they had grown; where they had learned about family, resilience, and love.

His bond with Chantelle was one of the most precious parts of his life. They had shared everything as children—their games, their secrets, their dreams. Even now, despite their differing paths, they remained close. He admired her intelligence, her discipline, and her quiet determination. She had a way of balancing their father's intensity and their mother's grace, embodying the best of both.

Jean-Pierre clenched his fists. He could not—would not—let this crisis destroy everything his family had built. If the crisis continued to spread; if the public turned against wine, and if their vineyard fell victim to the fear and disruption, it wouldn't just be a loss of income. It would be a loss of identity; of history, of everything that made them who they were.

He felt a surge of determination rise within him. He wouldn't let it happen. Not to his parents, not to

Chantelle, not to the generations who had come before them. He would stand resolute, defend their legacy, and prove himself worthy of being the heir to the Dupont name and the steward of their vineyard.

Jean-Pierre rose from his seat, his jaw set and his heart resolute. His family had faced challenges before, but this time was different. This time, the stakes were global, and the crisis loomed larger than ever. But he knew this much: they would face it as a unit, as a family, as they always had. And he would be the backbone they needed, unwavering in his love and loyalty to them all.

Chapter 25

The oak-panelled office of the Swiss President exuded a quiet gravitas, its walls lined with leather-bound books and portraits of past leaders. Marcel Dupont sat in a high-backed chair across from the President's imposing desk. The air was heavy with anticipation as the President, a tall, silver-haired man with piercing blue eyes, leaned forward, his clasped hands resting on the polished wood.

"Professor Dupont," he began, his voice steady but tinged with urgency. "Switzerland has always prided itself on its neutrality and innovation. But today, I call on you not as a Swiss citizen, but as a scientist of unparalleled brilliance. We face a crisis that extends beyond borders—a growing wave of inexplicable deaths. Your expertise may be the key to uncovering the truth."

Marcel inclined his head, his expression reserved. "I'm honoured by your words, Mr. President, but I'm not sure what assistance I can provide in this matter. My expertise lies in astrophysics and nuclear reactions, not public health."

The President nodded, acknowledging Marcel's humility.

"Precisely why you are the man we need. This crisis," he gestured toward a folder on his desk, "is not merely a matter of public health. It is a mystery rooted in science, one that could have far-reaching consequences if not resolved. I believe your background in particle physics, your pioneering work, and your deep understanding of atomic interactions make you uniquely qualified to lead this investigation."

Marcel's gaze drifted to the folder. Though he kept his demeanour composed, curiosity stirred within him. "What exactly are we dealing with?"

The President opened the folder and slid it across the desk. Photographs of young victims lay atop reports filled with dense text and medical jargon. Marcel picked up one of the images, studying the lifeless face of a young man.

"Drug overdose?" he asked.

"That's the official explanation," the President said, his voice grim. "But these deaths don't fit any known pattern. Minimal traces of drugs and alcohol are found in their systems, yet the physiological damage is catastrophic. Autopsies are inconclusive. And here's the truly troubling part—every victim so far had ingested both drugs and alcohol. It appears to be the common factor."

Marcel set the photo down, his mind racing. "Are there geographical patterns? Any commonalities beyond the substances?"

The President steepled his fingers. "Initially, the cases were sporadic. But over the past month, we've seen clusters in major cities—Zurich, Geneva, Basel—and similar reports are emerging worldwide. The phenomenon is escalating, Professor Dupont. If we don't act quickly, the consequences could be catastrophic."

Marcel leaned back in his chair, his sharp mind already analysing the data. "You believe this is more than a public health crisis. You're considering the possibility of an external agent—something engineered?"

The President's jaw tightened. "It's a possibility we can't ignore. If this is an act of bioterrorism or chemical warfare, we need answers—and fast. Your reputation precedes you, Professor Dupont. The groundbreaking research you led demonstrated an ability to unravel the most complex mysteries of the universe. This is no different, except the stakes are higher."

Marcel remained silent for a moment, the weight of the President's request settling heavily on him. "This isn't a task for one man," he finally said. "I'll need resources— a team."

"Anything you require," the President assured him. "But let me be clear—this mission demands discretion. The public must not know the full extent of what we suspect. Panic would only exacerbate the crisis."

Marcel nodded, his mind already assembling a mental list of potential collaborators. "I'll do what I can," he said, his voice firm. "But this will require expertise beyond my field."

The President's lips curved into a faint smile. "I trust you'll assemble the best. Time is of the essence, Professor Dupont. The world is counting on you."

Chapter 26

The morning sun poured into the kitchen of the Dupont chateau, casting a warm glow over the rustic stone walls and gleaming copper cookware. Chantelle sat at the wooden table, sipping a cup of coffee and flipping through her notes from the previous day's shift. The lines of fatigue on her face were softened by her quiet determination.

Marcel entered; his footsteps deliberate but unhurried. He carried a folder under his arm, his expression unreadable.

"Good morning, Chantelle," he greeted, his voice carrying a note of purpose.

She looked up, her green eyes sharp despite her exhaustion. "Morning, *Papa*. You're up early."

"I couldn't sleep," he admitted, setting the folder down on the table and taking a seat across from her. "There's something I need to discuss with you."

Chantelle arched an eyebrow, intrigued but cautious. "Sounds serious."

"It is," Marcel said, leaning forward. "I've been asked to lead an investigation into these unexplained deaths. The President himself believes I'm the right man for the job."

Chantelle's expression shifted to one of concern. "That's... incredible, but also daunting. What does he expect you to uncover?"

Marcel opened the folder, revealing the same photographs and reports he had reviewed earlier. He pushed them toward Chantelle. "Take a look."

She flipped through the documents, her brow furrowing as she absorbed the information. "These are the cases I've been dealing with," she said softly. "But why involve you?"

"Because this goes beyond medicine," Marcel explained. "The pattern suggests a scientific anomaly— something we don't yet understand. The victims had drugs and alcohol in their systems, but the reactions... They're unlike anything I've seen before."

Chantelle looked up, her gaze steady. "You think it's something chemical?"

"Perhaps," Marcel said. "Or biological. Or even radiological. That's what I intend to find out. But I can't do this alone, Chantelle. Your medical expertise is crucial."

Her eyes widened in surprise. "You want me to join you?"

"Yes," Marcel said simply. "You have an understanding of human physiology and patient care that I lack. I can analyse atoms, reactions, compounds—but I need someone who can interpret the human side of this crisis. I can't think of anyone better than you."

Chantelle hesitated the weight of his words sinking in. "This isn't just about science, is it? It's about lives—about stopping more deaths."

Marcel nodded; pride evident in his eyes. "Exactly. You've grown into an extraordinary woman, Chantelle. Your work at the hospital, your dedication—it's remarkable. And now, we have an opportunity to make a difference together."

She took a deep breath, her mind racing. "If I agree to this, it won't be easy. I'll need to balance my hospital shifts, and... what about confidentiality?"

"We'll work out the details," Marcel assured her. "But time is of the essence. Will you help me?"

After a moment of contemplation, Chantelle nodded. "Yes, *Papa*. I'll help."

* * *

Chantelle watched as her father left, the echo of his footsteps gradually fading down the hallway. The door clicked shut, leaving behind a stillness that felt unusually heavy. She remained seated at the kitchen table, the warmth of her father's presence still lingering. He had just entrusted her with an extraordinary responsibility, and the weight of his words seemed to vibrate in the silence of the empty kitchen.

Her father's voice still echoed in her mind: *"I can't do this alone, Chantelle. I need your insight, your sharpness, and your unique perspective. Together, we might just uncover what's happening and save lives."*

Chantelle drew in a deep breath and exhaled slowly, leaning back into the cushions. Her father's confidence in her stirred a blend of pride and trepidation. Marcel Dupont, the man chosen by the president to lead an investigation of international importance, had placed his trust in her.

Me, she thought, almost incredulously. *Of all people, he believes I can help solve this.*
But could she?

Her thoughts swirled like a storm, questions tumbling one over the other. What exactly was she walking into? What kind of evidence were they even looking for? How could her experience with the medical anomalies at the hospital contribute to solving something of this magnitude?

She leaned forward, resting her elbows on the table and cradling her head in her hands. A kaleidoscope of images from the hospital flashed through her mind—patients who had died inexplicably; their charts telling a story that simply didn't add up. She had heard the hushed conversations in the break room, the fragmented theories from colleagues who were as baffled as she was.

One of her coworkers, Dr. Lefevre, had once muttered under his breath, *"It's as if these patients are dying of nothing and everything all at once."*

She had initially dismissed his statement as hyperbolic frustration, but now it haunted her. Marcel's visit had breathed new life into those fragmented conversations, forcing her to reconsider. Were those inexplicable deaths just the tip of an iceberg, a symptom of something far larger and far more sinister?

She thought of the peculiarities she'd noticed in her few months on rotation. Patients whose bloodwork showed anomalies that didn't fit any known medical condition. Scans that revealed nothing abnormal but failed to explain the rapid deterioration of their health. And the whispers among her colleagues: Could this be a new, undetected pathogen? A biochemical agent? Or something even stranger?

And then there were the autopsies—no detectable signs of poisoning, no overdose levels of drugs, and no trace of foul play. Yet death hovered like an unrelenting spectre.

Chantelle reached for her notebook, where she had jotted down snippets of these anomalies. Flipping through the pages, she saw a list of recurring symptoms, some highlighted, others underlined. She paused at a note she had scrawled weeks ago:

"Commonality: drug and alcohol in system. No overdose levels. What is the catalyst?"

Her father's words suddenly resonated more clearly. The cases at her hospital weren't isolated incidents— they were puzzle pieces in a much larger, global picture. The magnitude of what Marcel was trying to uncover began to crystallize in her mind.

She put the notebook down and leaned back again, staring at the ceiling. A small smile crept across her face. Marcel's request had revealed something more than a plea for help—it had revealed his admiration for her work; for her capabilities. He had always been a stoic and exacting man, rarely offering praise without merit. That he had chosen to confide in her; to include her in such an important endeavour, was a testament to the respect he held for her.

Chantelle felt a deep sense of pride swelling within her. Her father's faith in her wasn't blind; it was rooted in years of watching her grow, work, and thrive.

He sees me, she thought. *Not just as his daughter, but as someone capable of making a difference.*

She thought of his unyielding intellect; his meticulous nature, and his unwavering determination. He had been selected by the president of their nation above all others. And now, he had chosen her.

If he believes in me, then I have to believe in myself too.

But the pride didn't drown out the enormity of the task. Instead, it seemed to amplify it. Her mind raced, trying to chart the path forward. She imagined the work involved—reviewing patient files, analysing patterns, and collaborating with medical, scientific, and government entities. It felt like staring into a labyrinth with no clear entrance.

Her thoughts flicked to the news broadcasts she had seen recently. The world was already on edge, with deaths rising and no clear answers in sight. If this investigation succeeded, it could save countless lives and restore hope to millions. But if they failed…

The idea of failure churned uneasily in her stomach. Yet, amid the uncertainty, she found herself drawn to the challenge. The possibility of making a global impact—of using her skills to contribute to something monumental—was both terrifying and exhilarating.

Chantelle stood and walked to the window, gazing out at the Alps in the background. Somewhere out there, people were unknowingly living under the shadow of this mysterious threat. And somewhere, her father was already working on a plan, meticulously piecing together a strategy.

Marcel Dupont was not a man who left anything to chance. He would lead with precision and care, ensuring every avenue was explored; every detail scrutinised. Chantelle took a deep breath, feeling the wave of uncertainty slowly give way to resolve.

Her father wasn't just asking for her help—he was inviting her to be part of something far greater than either of them. And despite the storm of thoughts swirling in her mind, she trusted him implicitly.

He'll lead us through this, she thought. *And I'll be ready to stand by his side.*

The weight of the moment settled over her shoulders like a mantle, but it wasn't a burden—it was a call to action. She pictured herself working alongside her father, contributing her medical expertise to unravel the mystery. She imagined the ripple effects of their success: fewer lives lost, families spared from grief, and a renewed sense of trust in science and humanity.

And above all, she imagined the pride in her father's eyes, knowing they had achieved something extraordinary together.

Chantelle's lips curved into a small, determined smile. The tsunami of thoughts in her mind began to calm, replaced by a quiet but steadfast confidence.

This is what I've worked for, she thought. *This is what I'm meant to do.*

As the morning sun strengthened, Chantelle turned back to her notebook, flipping to a fresh page. She began jotting down ideas, her handwriting quick and purposeful. Patterns, questions, potential leads—she wanted to be ready when the work began in earnest.

Her father had given her a choice, but in her heart, she knew there had never really been a question. She would stand with him, shoulder to shoulder, and do everything in her power to solve this mystery.

Her father's trust had ignited a spark, and now it burned brightly, illuminating the path ahead.

"Let's do this," she whispered to herself, her resolve unshakable.

* * *

In the quiet sanctuary of her laboratory, Genevieve was meticulously arranging a series of test tubes when Marcel entered. The familiar scent of antiseptic and chemicals filled the air, mingling with the faint aroma of lavender from the garden outside.

"Genevieve," Marcel said softly, his voice cutting through the stillness.

She turned, a smile breaking across her face. "Marcel. What brings you here?"

He approached her workbench, his expression serious. "I need your help."

Genevieve paused as she looked at him curiously. "What kind of help?"

Marcel explained the situation, recounting his meeting with the President and his conversation with Chantelle.

 Genevieve listened intently, her scientific mind already piecing together possibilities.
"This is... extraordinary," she said when he finished. "But why me?"

"Because you're the best molecular scientist I know," Marcel said without hesitation. "Your work on encapsulation and chemical preservation is unparalleled. If there's anyone who can help unravel this mystery, it's you."

Genevieve regarded him for a moment, her eyes searching his face. "You're serious about this."

"Deadly serious," Marcel said. "I can't do this without you, Genevieve. We've always been strongest when we work together."

Her lips curved into a small smile. "Just like old times, then?"

"Exactly," Marcel said, a hint of nostalgia in his voice. "Like the university, like Chornobyl."

Genevieve's expression softened as memories flooded back. "Those were different days, Marcel. But if you think I can contribute, I'm with you."

Marcel's relief was appreciable. "Thank you, Genevieve. Together, I believe we can solve this."

They shared a moment of quiet resolve, and their complementary skills and shared history would form the foundation of their renewed partnership.

The door closed with a soft click as Marcel left her laboratory, his footsteps retreating outside down the path.

Genevieve remained seated in her chair, her fingers loosely entwined in front of her, her gaze fixed on the antique desk in front of her but seeing far beyond it. His words still resonated in the air, heavy with gravity and laced with trust.

"Genevieve, I need you. There's no one else I trust more to help me navigate this."

It wasn't the first time Marcel had sought her counsel or leaned on her expertise. Throughout their lives, they had been a team—an unshakable partnership rooted in mutual respect, love, and an unwavering belief in each other's brilliance. But this was different. The president himself had turned to Marcel, entrusting him with unravelling a mystery that seemed to defy logic and science alike.

Genevieve exhaled slowly, leaning back in her chair. She closed her eyes, letting the silence settle around her. The president. *The President of Switzerland.* The enormity of the task weighed on her shoulders; yet it was pride—profound, unshakable pride that dominated her thoughts.

Her mind began to turn over the implications. The deaths, the unanswered questions, the worldwide panic—it wasn't just a scientific challenge; it was a humanitarian crisis. And at its heart stood Marcel. The enormity of the task was daunting, but her pride for her husband outweighed her fear.

She thought back to their conversation moments ago. The determination in Marcel's voice, the way his eyes had gleamed with focus despite the weight he bore. He had been chosen for this—not just for his expertise but for his ability to see beyond the surface, to connect dots others might miss.

"Why Marcel?" she whispered aloud, her voice soft in the quiet room.

The question lingered for a moment before the answer came flooding in.

Her thoughts turned to his achievements, a timeline of brilliance that began at university. She could still picture him as a young man—intense, driven, and unapologetically passionate about physics. He had been magnetic, drawing others into his orbit with his sharp intellect and unyielding curiosity.

At university, he had been a pioneer, working on projects that pushed the boundaries of human understanding. His contributions to particle physics had earned him respect and admiration across the scientific community. And then there were the lectures—dozens of them—delivered to packed halls where students and peers alike hung on his every word. Marcel had a gift, not just for understanding the complexities of the universe but for communicating them with clarity and passion.

Genevieve smiled faintly, a rush of pride warming her chest. It wasn't just his accomplishments that defined him, but the integrity and humility with which he approached his work. He had never sought fame or recognition; his focus had always been on the pursuit of knowledge and the betterment of humanity.

Her smile deepened as her thoughts shifted to their time at university. Those early years had been a whirlwind of discovery, both academically and personally. They had been drawn to each other not just by love but by a shared passion for science. She remembered late nights in the lab, their heads bent over experiments, their laughter breaking the silence as they teased each other over miscalculations or celebrated breakthroughs.

They had been a formidable team even then, their strengths complementing each other perfectly. Marcel's analytical mind had a way of seeing patterns where others saw confusion, while her meticulous approach ensured no detail was overlooked. Together, they had achieved more than either could have alone.

Even after their careers had taken them in different directions, their partnership had remained steadfast. They had supported each other's endeavours, offering insights, feedback, and unwavering encouragement. Marcel had always valued her perspective, often saying she had a way of seeing what he couldn't—a testament to the deep respect they shared.

Now, as she sat in the quiet of their study, Genevieve realised this was the moment they had been preparing for all their lives. This was the time to combine their strengths, to work as one, not just as husband and wife but as partners in the truest sense of the word.

Her thoughts turned back to the present, to the crisis that had prompted the president's call. The deaths weren't just numbers on a chart; they were lives lost, families shattered, and communities grieving. This was bigger than science or personal ambition—it was about humanity.

Genevieve felt a surge of determination. This wasn't just Marcel's moment to shine; it was theirs. Together, they had the skills, the knowledge, and the experience to make a difference. She could feel the weight of responsibility pressing down on her, but it was a weight she was willing to bear.

She rose from her chair and moved to the window, looking out at the vineyard bathed in the rays of the morning sun. The rows of vines stretched out before her, a testament to the life they had built with each other.

This place was their sanctuary, their legacy. And now, it was also a reminder of what was at stake. Genevieve thought of Marcel again, of his unrelenting determination and his ability to rise to any challenge.

"This is your time, Marcel," she murmured, her voice steady. "I know you can do this, my love. And I'll stand right beside you."

The enormity of the task ahead didn't diminish her resolve. If anything, it strengthened it. She thought of the lives they could save; the suffering they could prevent. This wasn't just about solving a mystery; it was about making a tangible difference in the world.

Her mind began to race, piecing together the steps they would need to take. There were so many variables, so many questions to answer. But Genevieve knew that as a team, they could find the truth.

As the midday sun approached, Genevieve felt a sense of clarity settle over her. This was what she and Marcel had always been meant to do. Their journey had led them here, to this moment, where their skills, experiences, and love for each other would be tested like never before.

They were a team, and they would face this challenge united, just as they always had.

Genevieve turned away from the window and returned to the desk, her mind already brimming with ideas. The path ahead wouldn't be easy, but she was ready to take the first step.

For Marcel. For their family. For the world.

* * *

Marcel emerged from Genevieve's laboratory, his mind a whirlwind of thoughts. The gravity of the investigation weighed heavily on him, but he felt a sliver of relief knowing that Genevieve and Chantelle had agreed to join his team. Now, there was one more person he needed to speak with—his son, Jean-Pierre.

Making his way to the winery; Marcel called out; his voice echoing through the stone walls. "Jean-Pierre? Are you here?" He checked each corner of the winery, scanning the rows of barrels, the bottling area, and the storage rooms, but there was no sign of his son.

Frowning, Marcel stepped outside, shielding his eyes against the late afternoon sun. The golden light bathed the vineyard in a warm glow, the rows of vines stretching out in perfect symmetry toward the horizon. He called again, his voice carrying across the expanse.

"Jean-Pierre!"

This time, a faint response came from the far end of the vineyard. Marcel followed the sound, weaving through the rows of vines until he spotted his son crouched near a rose bush at the end of one row.

Jean-Pierre stood as Marcel approached, brushing dirt from his hands. "Ah, there you are, *Papa*," he said with a broad smile. "Just checking the early warning system." He gestured to the rosebushes planted at the ends of each row. "You know, the roses are like sentinels. They show signs of disease or pests before the vines do. If these are healthy; it's a good sign for the vineyard."

Marcel forced a smile, nodding at his son's enthusiastic explanation. He admired Jean-Pierre's dedication, his deep connection to the land, and his thoughtful approach to preserving their legacy. But today, Marcel had more pressing matters to discuss.

"Jean-Pierre," Marcel began, his tone more serious now. "I need to talk to you about something important."

Jean-Pierre's smile faded as he noticed the weight in his father's voice. "What is it, Papa?" he asked, his hazel eyes filled with concern.

Marcel took a deep breath, steadying himself.

"I've been approached by the president of Switzerland." He paused, letting the gravity of the statement sink in. "He has tasked me with leading an investigation—an investigation that is both confidential and of the utmost importance in dealing with a current global crisis."

Jean-Pierre's eyes widened, his mind racing. The president? He thought of the recent news bulletins, the rising disorder, and the implications of the mysterious deaths Chantelle had mentioned. The world was in turmoil, and now his father was at the centre of it.

"I've already asked your mother and Chantelle to join my core team," Marcel continued. "Their expertise is essential for the scientific and medical aspects of the investigation. But I need you too, Jean-Pierre, though in a different capacity."

Jean-Pierre leaned forward; his breath held in anticipation.

"I need you to hold the fort," Marcel said, his voice steady but tinged with urgency. "The vineyard, the winery—our family's legacy—it's all in your hands now. While we are consumed by this investigation; someone needs to ensure that everything here runs smoothly; that the business remains strong. More importantly, I need you to keep the family grounded."

Jean-Pierre listened intently, his heart swelling with a mix of pride and responsibility. His father had always been a towering figure in his life—respected, admired, and often, a source of inspiration. To hear that Marcel was entrusting him with such a vital role filled Jean-Pierre with a profound sense of purpose.

Marcel placed a hand on his son's shoulder. "Jean-Pierre, I don't know what we're walking into. This investigation—it's already overwhelming, and we've only just begun. I need your help to ensure that the family remains strong and united. We will be stretched thin, but knowing that you are here, taking care of things, will allow us to focus on the task ahead."

Jean-Pierre's throat tightened, but he managed a firm nod. "
Papa, you can count on me," he said, his voice steady despite the storm of emotions within him. "I will take care of the vineyard, the winery, and the family. You don't need to worry about anything here."

Marcel's eyes softened, a rare moment of vulnerability breaking through his usually composed demeanour.

"Thank you, my son. This means more to me than you can imagine."

Jean-Pierre stepped closer, his hands gripping his father's shoulders. "And, Papa," he added with a reassuring shake, "if you need anything—anything at all—don't hesitate to ask. I'm here for you, for *Maman*, for Chantelle. We're a family, and we'll get through this as a family."

Marcel smiled, a flicker of relief passing over his face. "Thank you, Jean-Pierre," he said quietly. "I know I can rely on you."

As they stood side by side at the edge of the vineyard, the sun dipping low on the horizon, Jean-Pierre felt a renewed sense of resolve. The vineyard was more than just a business—it was their home, their heritage, and their sanctuary. He would protect it with everything he had, not just for himself, but for his family.

And in that moment, Marcel knew he had made the right choice.

Chapter 27

The Dupont family gathered in the laboratory that Marcel had converted from an old cellar on the estate some time ago for Genevieve. The stone walls held the chill of the early morning, and the air buzzed with quiet anticipation. A whiteboard dominated one wall, already filled with Marcel's neat handwriting and diagrams, while stacks of reports, case files, and medical charts were spread across a long wooden table.

Marcel stood at the head of the room, his stance commanding but approachable; the weight of the task ahead etched subtly into his features. He gestured toward a corner of the lab where a sleek, state-of-the-art communication terminal stood next to an encrypted laptop and a secure phone line.

"Before we begin," he said, his voice steady but resolute, "there's something you both should know. I've established a direct protocol with the president's office.

We've been allocated a government official on standby, someone with clearance and authority to provide us with immediate access to records, autopsy reports, chemical databases, and any other resources we require."

Genevieve raised an eyebrow, impressed. Chantelle, leaning against the table's edge, folded her arms, intrigued.

"Who's the liaison?" Chantelle asked.

"A man named Henri Morel," Marcel replied. "He's a senior operative within the intelligence division, well-versed in maintaining discretion. His job is to assist us without delay, ensuring we have what we need without raising suspicion. But"—he paused, his gaze sweeping over both of them—"I've made it clear that, for now, this investigation remains within our core team. Henri is to serve as a facilitator, not a participant."

Genevieve nodded thoughtfully, her fingers brushing the edge of a report on the table. "That's wise. We need to establish a clear and solid foundation before involving anyone else. If we prematurely share incomplete findings, it could lead to misunderstandings—or worse, leaks."

"Precisely," Marcel agreed. "The president has emphasised that discretion and containment are paramount. Public panic would be catastrophic, and until we have definitive answers, this investigation must stay contained." He paused and looked at his two ladies. Then he added, "And that is why I will keep it to the core team. Us. I cannot trust anyone else right now.

He turned toward the whiteboard, picking up a marker. "Our first task is to establish the basics—a comprehensive database of chemical compounds for all substances involved. This includes every drug we suspect might be linked to the deaths, every type of alcohol identified in autopsy reports, and the chemical elements found in the victims' samples."

Genevieve stepped forward, her mind already racing. "We'll need to analyse every potential reaction, every bond, and every anomaly. If there's a pattern, it will emerge once we've mapped everything out."

"Exactly," Marcel said. "We can't afford to work in fragments. This has to be a methodical, unified effort. Only once we've established a base can we begin to draw conclusions and test hypotheses."

Chantelle straightened, her medical instincts kicking in. "I'll focus on the autopsy reports and medical charts. If there are patterns in the physiological reactions, we might be able to correlate them with specific chemical triggers."

Marcel gave her a small smile, his pride evident. "That's why I need you, Chantelle. Your insight into the human body and your experience with these cases will be invaluable."

"And what about the drugs and the alcohol?" Genevieve asked, her tone measured.

Marcel nodded. "We'll examine them alongside everything else. We need to break them down to every single chemical element. With a base we can then rule out—or confirm—any link between specific elements.

For now, we work without assumptions and from the base up."

Genevieve and Chantelle exchanged a glance, a shared understanding passing between them. This was no ordinary investigation. It was a convergence of their individual expertise, a task that required not just intellect but unwavering trust in one another.

Marcel's voice broke the silence. "This isn't going to be easy. The scale of what we're attempting is immense, and the stakes couldn't be higher. But if there's anyone who can do this, it's us. Together as a team."

Chantelle stepped closer to the table, picking up a stack of medical charts. "Let's get started, then."

Genevieve followed suit, her fingers grazing the cold surface of the lab equipment she knew so well. "We'll need to set up distinct workstations for each area of analysis. I'll take the chemical compounds and start cataloguing them against all molecular structures."

Marcel watched them with quiet satisfaction. Despite the gravity of the situation, there was something reassuring about seeing his family united in purpose. They were stepping into the unknown, but they weren't doing it alone.

Over the next few hours, the lab hummed with activity. Chantelle buried herself in medical reports, her face lined with concentration as she sifted through autopsy findings, noting any recurring anomalies. Genevieve meticulously recorded data, her hands steady as she worked with vials and reagents, her mind sharp as she cross-referenced chemical properties.

Marcel moved between them, offering guidance and answering questions, but mostly observing with a sense of awe. This wasn't just a team—it was his family. And as the morning turned to afternoon, the Duponts began to uncover the first threads of a mystery that would test everything they knew.

For Marcel, Genevieve, and Chantelle, this wasn't just about solving a crisis. It was about proving, once again, that together, they could overcome anything.

Marcel returned from the kitchen with a fresh pot of coffee and a jug of Genevieve's homemade lemonade. He topped up the girl's glasses and poured himself a fresh cup of espresso. Genevieve adjusted her lab coat, her fingers methodically straightening her gloves as she prepared to delve into the few samples they had managed to collect thus far. Chantelle stood nearby, flipping through her patient notes, her brow furrowed in concentration. Marcel, ever the methodical leader, returned to the head of the table, his sharp hazel eyes scanning the data.

"Remember, we need to approach this systematically," Marcel reminded them; his voice calm but authoritative. "First, we isolate each variable. Drugs, alcohol, and specific affected organs within the human body, each to be examined separately. Once the baseline is established, if nothing surfaces, we move to combinations."

Genevieve nodded, her tone pragmatic. "And we can't overlook environmental factors. Could there be contaminants? Reactions triggered by external conditions?"

"Possibly," Marcel agreed, picking up a marker. "But let's start with what we know." He drew three interconnected circles on the whiteboard, labelling them:

Drugs, *Alcohol*, and *Human Physiology*.
"We'll test each category in isolation. Chantelle, you'll stick to and focus on patient histories. Genevieve, you handle the chemical compositions and breakdown of all the drugs. I'll work on alcohol analysis."

Chantelle nodded, her face set with quiet determination. "I'll cross-reference the symptoms with the autopsy reports. Maybe there's something subtle we may overlook."

The hours stretched on as they immersed themselves in their respective tasks. Chantelle pored over the hospital files, her green eyes scanning every detail, searching for patterns in the confusion. Marcel analysed the molecular structures of various alcohol samples, his movements precise as he worked under the glow of the microscope. Genevieve's focus was unwavering as she studied the chemical makeup of confiscated drugs, her hands steady as she documented each finding.

By evening, the whiteboard was filled with notes and diagrams, but the results were frustratingly inconclusive.

"No anomalies in the drugs," Genevieve reported, her voice tinged with weariness as she removed her gloves. "Everything matches standard compositions."

"Same with the alcohol," Marcel said, rubbing his temple. "No signs of adulteration or contamination."

Chantelle sighed, setting down a file. "And the autopsies show nothing definitive. Just the same cascade of organ failure. No clear link."

Marcel leaned against the table; his gaze distant. "It's as if the combination of drugs and alcohol somehow triggers the effect. But why? What's the mechanism?"

Genevieve crossed her arms, her expression thoughtful. "Can we move to combinations? What if we test the substances together? Simulate real-world conditions?" Marcel straightened, a spark of determination lighting his eyes. "That's our next step, but let's ensure that all base elements have been identified and documented. Then we'll recreate the circumstances under controlled conditions. If there's an interaction, we'll find it."

Chantelle hesitated, her voice cautious. "But this also means we're delving into unknown territory. If the combination is dangerous..."

Marcel placed a reassuring hand on her shoulder. "We'll take every precaution. But we have to push forward. Too many lives are at stake. I'm used to taking precautions. I learnt that very well during some of my most complex projects."

As night fell, the family prepared for the next phase of their investigation, their resolve unwavering despite the uncertainty ahead.

Chapter 28

Across Switzerland and beyond, the drug underworld was unravelling. News reports chronicled a startling rise in fatalities among known gang members, particularly those linked to the drug trade. Cartels that once operated with impunity now faced a crisis that no amount of money or muscle could fix.

In the dimly lit basement of a Zurich nightclub, a group of cartel leaders convened. The room was tense, the air heavy with the acrid smell of cigarette smoke.

"We're losing people faster than we can count," growled one man, his scarred face twisted in anger. "Every shipment, every deal—it's as if death follows our product."

A younger member, his hands trembling slightly, spoke up. "It's not just us. Rivals are dropping too. Whatever this is, it's not targeted."

"Not targeted?" another voice barked, slamming a fist on the table. "It's decimating our operations! Someone is behind this—a rival cartel, the police, maybe even the government!"

The room erupted in heated accusations and frantic speculation. Some pointed fingers at rival gangs, accusing them of sabotage. Others muttered darkly about chemical weapons and conspiracies; their paranoia fuelled by the unrelenting wave of deaths.

Meanwhile, on the streets, the impact was even more visible. Dealers abandoned their corners, terrified of handling the tainted drugs. Users; once loyal customers, avoided their usual haunts, whispering about friends who had taken a hit and never woken up. The once-thriving drug trade was collapsing under the weight of fear and uncertainty.

In Geneva, a drive-by shooting left four men dead, their bodies sprawled in the street. Police cordoned off the area as reporters swarmed, their cameras capturing the grim scene. The headlines the next day declared it a turf war, but the reality was far more complex.

At the heart of the mayhem was Don Paolo, one of Europe's most notorious drug lords. Seated in his lavish villa overlooking Lake Geneva, he listened as his lieutenants detailed the latest losses. His normally composed demeanour was fraying at the edges, his dark eyes flashing with frustration.

"We can't sustain this," one of his men admitted, his voice low. "The product is poisoned. The buyers don't trust us. And the killings... It's destroying our reputation."

Don Paolo leaned back in his chair, his fingers steepled. "This isn't just bad luck," he said coldly. "Someone is trying to dismantle us—systematically and efficiently. We need to find out who."

But even as the cartels scrambled for answers, the deaths continued. Hospitals reported an influx of young men and women with the same baffling symptoms: sudden organ failure, no clear cause. Law enforcement agencies were inundated with cases; their resources stretched thin as they tried to stem the tide of violence and loss.

Back at the chateau, Marcel watched the news with a grim expression. Chantelle sat beside him; her hands clasped tightly in her lap.

"The cartels are imploding," she said quietly. "But at what cost? These are human lives, Papa."

Marcel nodded; his voice heavy. "I know, Chantelle. And the longer this goes unsolved, the more lives will be lost—on both sides of the law."

Genevieve entered the room, her face pale but resolute. "I've set up the next phase of the experiments," she said. "We'll start tomorrow."

Marcel turned to her; his eyes filled with determination. "Then let's make tomorrow count. We're running out of time."

As the night deepened, the Dupont family prepared to continue their quest for answers, knowing that the stakes had never been higher.

Chapter 29

Marcel sat in his study, the room bathed in the soft glow of his antique desk lamp. The air was thick with the scent of aged wood and the faint, comforting aroma of the vineyard wafting through the open window. He had been pouring over his notes for hours, the pages covered in his precise handwriting, mathematical equations, and sketches of molecular diagrams. Yet the solution still eluded him.

In frustration, he leaned back in his chair and gazed at the ceiling, his mind racing through the possibilities. The symptoms, the patterns, the sheer inexplicability of the deaths—they all pointed to something beyond the ordinary. Something in the interaction between the drugs and alcohol was triggering a reaction, but why?

His thoughts drifted back to his work at university. Antimatter, the elusive twin of matter, had always fascinated him. It was unpredictable, volatile, and immensely powerful. Could the deaths be linked to something as fundamental as subatomic particles? He shook his head, dismissing the idea as too far-fetched. But the thought lingered.

He pulled out a file containing data from the autopsies and laboratory analyses. Traces of radiation had been found in some of the samples, though not at levels high enough to be immediately harmful. It was puzzling, almost as if the radiation was a ghost—present but intangible.

"Antimatter and radiation…" Marcel muttered, leaning forward again. He sketched a new diagram, illustrating the interaction of molecular compounds with radioactive isotopes. His pen moved swiftly across the paper, the lines connecting in a web of hypotheses.

The more he worked, the clearer the picture became. Radiation, when combined with certain molecular structures, could destabilize the atomic bonds. The resulting reaction could create a cascade of cellular destruction—explaining the rapid organ failure observed in the victims.

Marcel's heart quickened. If the drugs contained trace amounts of radioactive contamination, even a small interaction with alcohol could trigger a catastrophic reaction. It was a long shot, but it was the first hypothesis that made sense.

Marcel leaned back in his chair, his mind drifting to the haunting days he and Genevieve spent in Chornobyl. He remembered analysing the lingering effects of radiation exposure on the environment; observing how it destabilised molecular bonds in the soil and water. The patterns had been stark—small changes in atomic structure leading to catastrophic results. Those findings, etched in his memory, now resurfaced with chilling clarity.

The connection was undeniable. What he had witnessed in Chornobyl's contaminated zones echoed the effects he was piecing together now. If radiation was indeed part of the equation, its destabilising influence on molecular bonds could explain the inexplicable deaths. His gut tightened as the implications deepened. This wasn't just about science; it was about harnessing everything he had learned to prevent further tragedy.

He was interrupted by the sound of footsteps. Genevieve appeared in the doorway, her expression one of concern and curiosity.

"You've been here all night," she said gently, crossing the room to stand beside him. "Any progress?"

Marcel gestured to his notes, his excitement barely contained. "I think I've found something. Look—radiation. It's the missing piece. What if the contamination is so subtle that it's only detectable when combined with certain chemicals?"

Genevieve didn't know why but she felt uneasy. She frowned, studying his notes. "That would explain the unpredictability of the deaths. But where would the radiation come from?" Genevieve hesitated for a second, feeling even more uneasy.

Marcel also hesitated, his mind racing. "It could be an environmental contaminant. Or…" He trailed off, a shadow passing over his face. The thought was too troubling to voice aloud.

Genevieve placed a hand on his shoulder. "I don't like the sound of your voice, Marcel. You're scaring me." She caught her breath and continued, "You may be onto something, Marcel. But before we jump to conclusions, we need to confirm it. Let's run some tests tomorrow."

Marcel nodded, his resolve hardening. "If this is the answer, it's only the beginning. We need to find the source—and fast." He tried to remain brave and resolute.

* * *

The next morning, Chantelle joined her parents in the laboratory. The tension in the room was felt by each one of them as Marcel and Genevieve explained their latest findings. Chantelle listened intently, her sharp mind processing the information with precision. The word radiation did not trigger anything in her mind like it did her parents.

"So you think radiation is the trigger?" she asked, her voice steady.

Marcel nodded. "It's a theory, but it fits the data. We're preparing to test it now."

Chantelle's forehead creased, her thoughts turning to her patients. "If that's true, there must be a common factor among the victims. Something that links them beyond just the drugs and alcohol."

She retrieved her notebook, flipping to the section where she had meticulously documented her observations. "Many of the patients showed similar symptoms—nausea, dizziness, rapid organ failure. But there was one thing that stood out to me. In almost every case of the more recent ones, the victims had consumed high-proof alcohol shortly before their deaths."

Genevieve raised an eyebrow. "High proof? That's interesting. It would amplify any chemical reaction, especially one involving radiation."

Chantelle nodded, her mind racing. "Exactly. And there's another pattern. Most of the drugs involved in these cases were synthetic. Could the manufacturing process of drugs or alcohol be introducing contaminants?"

Marcel leaned forward; his hazel eyes alight with interest. "Synthetic drugs would be more susceptible to contamination during production. If even a small amount of radioactive material was introduced…"

He paused, his mind jumping to the preservative pills Genevieve had been developing. A pang of unease shot through him, but he quickly dismissed it. There was no evidence linking the pills to the deaths—at least, not yet.

Chantelle continued, unaware of her father's inner turmoil. "I also noticed that the victims were all heavy users. It's almost as if their bodies were primed for a reaction."

Genevieve glanced at Marcel. "That would make sense. Chronic exposure could weaken the body's defences, making them more vulnerable to any external trigger."

Chantelle closed her notebook, her expression resolute. "We need to focus on the drugs. If the contamination is coming from the manufacturing process, we might be able to trace it back to the source."

Marcel nodded, a sense of pride swelling in his chest. His daughter's insights were invaluable, her medical expertise complementing his own scientific knowledge. "You're right, Chantelle. Let's divide the work. Genevieve and I will continue analysing the chemical reactions. You focus on the patient histories. If we can find a link, it might lead us to the answer."

As they worked, the pieces of the puzzle began to fall into place. Chantelle's meticulous research uncovered a striking pattern: many of the victims had purchased their drugs from the same supplier. Meanwhile, Marcel and Genevieve's experiments confirmed that the combination of alcohol and certain synthetic compounds could amplify the effects of radiation.

By the end of the day, they had a breakthrough. Chantelle discovered that one of the suppliers was based near a facility known for handling radioactive materials. It was a tenuous connection, but it was enough to reignite their determination.

As the family gathered in the living room that evening, exhaustion gave way to a renewed sense of purpose. They were closer than ever to solving the mystery, but the road ahead was still fraught with uncertainty.

Marcel raised his right hand thumb-up; his gaze sweeping over his wife and daughter. "To progress," he said, his voice filled with quiet determination. "We're not there yet, but we're getting closer."

Chantelle smiled, her green eyes shining with hope. "And to family. We're stronger together."

As they comforted each other, the gravity of their task hung heavy in the air.

The mystery was unravelling, but the full truth had yet to reveal itself.

Chapter 30

The dining room at the Dupont family's chateau was usually a sanctuary—a place for laughter, discussion, and the sharing of ideas. Tonight, however, the atmosphere was taut. The smothered glow of the chandelier cast shadows across the room, reflecting the unease that simmered beneath the surface.

Marcel sat at the head of the table, his posture rigid, a glass of red wine in hand. To his left, Genevieve delicately cut into her plate of coq au vin, her movements precise but distracted. Across from her, Chantelle sat with her arms crossed, her green eyes focused intently on her father. Jean-Pierre, the family's quiet observer, occupied his usual seat, his brow furrowed as he sensed the undercurrents of conflict.

The conversation had started innocuously enough—an update from Jean-Pierre on the vineyard's progress and a brief exchange between Marcel and Genevieve about their ongoing experiments. But Chantelle, driven by a growing sense of urgency, had shifted the focus to the deaths she'd been witnessing at the hospital.

"I'm telling you, Papa, the patterns are unmistakable," she said, her voice steady but laced with frustration. "These aren't random deaths. There's something linking them—something we're not seeing."

Marcel sighed, placing his glass down with deliberate care. "Chantelle, I understand your concerns. But we're investigating as thoroughly as we can. These things take time."

"Time we don't have," she shot back. "The death toll is rising every day. People are terrified. The scientific community is grasping at straws, and meanwhile, we're sitting here, eating dinner as if nothing is happening."

Genevieve's fork clinked against her plate as she set it down, her expression calm but wary. "Chantelle, your father isn't dismissing this. We're all doing our part to find answers."

"But it's not enough," Chantelle insisted, her voice rising. "Every day I see families destroyed, lives lost—and for what? Because we're too careful? Too afraid to take risks?"

Marcel's jaw tightened, his hazel eyes meeting his daughter's fiery gaze. "Enough, Chantelle. This is not about fear. It's about precision. We cannot afford to make mistakes."

Chantelle leaned forward, her expression imploring. "And what about the human cost, Papa? What about the lives that could be saved if we act now?"

Jean-Pierre, sensing the tension escalating, interjected cautiously. "Perhaps we need to focus on immediate actions while continuing the investigation. Chantelle's perspective is valid, Papa. She's seeing the impact firsthand."

Marcel looked at his son, his expression softening slightly. "Jean-Pierre, I understand the urgency. But science is not a race. It's a methodical pursuit of truth. One misstep could lead to even greater consequences."

Genevieve reached for Marcel's hand, her touch grounding him. "We all want the same thing," she said gently. "Let's not lose sight of that."

Chantelle exhaled sharply, leaning back in her chair. "I just don't know how much longer we can wait," she said quietly, her voice heavy with exhaustion.

The room fell silent, the weight of her words settling over them. Marcel glanced at Genevieve; his thoughts conflicted. He understood his daughter's frustration, but his instincts told him to tread carefully.

As the family finished their meal in strained silence; the tension remained unspoken but noticeable. The dinner ended, but the fractures in their unity lingered, a reminder of the growing stakes and the toll it was taking on them all.

* * *

Later that night, Marcel found Genevieve in her study. The room was dimly lit, with papers and scientific journals spread across her desk. She sat with her head in her hands, her usually composed demeanour visibly shaken.

"Genevieve," Marcel said softly, stepping into the room.

She looked up, her dark eyes glistening with unshed tears.
"I think Chantelle is right," she said, her voice barely above a whisper. "We can't keep hiding from the truth."

Marcel crossed the room and sat beside her, his gaze steady. "What truth?"
Genevieve hesitated, her hands trembling as she reached for a folder on her desk. She opened it to reveal a series of lab reports, her neat handwriting filling the margins with notes.

"It has to be the preservatives," she admitted, her voice breaking. "I didn't realise it at first, but... I think they're the source of the contamination."

Marcel's breath caught, his mind racing. "How? How could that be possible?"

Genevieve looked away, worried and somewhat terrified. She picked up the pair of her personal inner gloves lying on the table next to her. "The gloves," she said, her voice barely audible. She fondled the gloves uncomfortably in her hands and continued, "The ones I used at Chornobyl. I've racked my brain and traced every step over and over. What if there were trace amounts of radioactive material embedded in the fabric? What if I introduced radioactive material into the pills? They were the only common piece of clothing or equipment that I used in Chornobyl and in my lab."

Marcel stared at her, his mind reeling. The implications were staggering. "Genevieve… this means…"

She nodded, tears spilling down her cheeks. "I've been using those gloves while handling the ingredients for the pills. If they are contaminated, then I could be responsible. And now it's out there, in the alcohol, in the drugs, in the deaths …"

Marcel leaned back, his hands running through his hair. The weight of her revelation pressed down on him, threatening to crush him. "Genevieve, this changes everything. If this is true. If this gets out…"

"I know," she whispered, her voice filled with anguish. "I cannot believe it *mon cher*, but it is a possibility, Marcel. The minute you mentioned radiation, Chornobyl sprung to mind. I'm scared, Marcel." Her voice trailed off, and the tears ran down her cheek.

Marcel took her hands in his, his grip firm. "We will do a thorough investigation of all your clothing, including and especially the gloves plus all equipment, and inspect the whole laboratory," he said, his voice resolute. "We'll retrace every step; draw a timeline. We will be absolutely clear about everything, every step of the way. We will leave no stone unturned."

Genevieve shook her head, tears streaming down her face. "How? The contamination is already spreading. People are dying, possibly because of me."

Marcel cupped her face in his hands, forcing her to meet his gaze. "Because of us," he corrected. "We're in this together, Genevieve. And we'll find the true cause and the true source. Don't jump to conclusions."

Genevieve nodded, her resolve strengthening. "We have to. For Chantelle, for Jean-Pierre—for everyone."

Marcel pulled her into an embrace; the weight of their shared burden pressing down on them. The road ahead was uncertain, but as a couple; they would face it.

As they sat in the quiet of the study, Marcel's mind began to race. He knew that he had to uncover every stone and that he needed to provide solid proof. It was daunting. What if it was them? He knew that it was going to be challenging, but it was also a step closer to understanding the mystery. And in understanding, there was hope for a solution.

* * *

The following day, in the dim light of the laboratory, the private, secure phone on the counter rang, its sharp tone cutting through the silence. Marcel froze, the sound startling him from his thoughts. For a moment, he stared at the device, not expecting it to ring, and its existence was a stark reminder of the high-stakes investigation he had been thrust into.

Genevieve glanced up from her notes, her fear renewed as her face was riddled with concern. Marcel hesitated, then stepped toward the phone. Taking a deep breath, he lifted the receiver and answered.

"Marcel speaking," he said, his voice steady despite the flutter of apprehension in his chest.

A familiar voice responded, calm and formal. "Henri here. The president asked me to follow up and check that all is in order."

Marcel exhaled silently, nodding as if Henri could see him. "Ah, yes. Thank you for checking in," he replied. "The wheels are in motion. We've formulated a detailed work plan to establish a baseline for our investigation. We're ensuring that no stone is left unturned."

Henri's tone softened but carried the weight of the president's authority. "Good to hear, Marcel. The president wanted me to remind you of the gravity of the situation and the importance of the matter. He has full confidence in you—he believes you're the right man for the job."

Marcel's grip on the receiver tightened. "I appreciate the president's confidence," he said carefully, choosing his words with precision. "I've assembled a core team, and we're fully engaged in the investigation. Rest assured, we understand the significance of this task."

Henri paused, his next words deliberate. "The president also emphasized the need for discretion. Premature conclusions could lead to widespread panic. Containing information to your core team is crucial until you have definitive findings."

"Understood," Marcel replied firmly. "We're taking every precaution to ensure that preliminary information remains within the team. The integrity of this investigation is my top priority."

"Very well, Professor," Henri said, his tone lightening slightly. "The president and I wish you well. Now, tell me—are you secure from a safety standpoint? Is there anything you require?"

Marcel glanced around the laboratory, his gaze settling on Genevieve, who watched him intently. He hesitated, considering the offer, then replied, "We're secure for now. I don't want to attract unnecessary attention by increasing our visible presence. Discretion is as much about subtlety as containment."

Henri seemed to consider this before replying, "Understood, Marcel. If circumstances change, don't hesitate to reach out."

"I'll contact you when I have specific requirements," Marcel assured him. "For now, we have what we need." "Very well. Good luck, Professor," Henri said before the line clicked and the call ended.

Marcel replaced the receiver with a sense of resolve. He turned to Genevieve, who raised an eyebrow. "That was Henri," he explained. "The president wanted to ensure we're on track and reminded us of the importance of discretion."

Genevieve nodded. "We already knew that, but it's good to hear they trust you."

Marcel's expression hardened. "It's more than trust—it's pressure. But we'll rise to it. We don't have a choice."

Genevieve placed a hand on his arm. "And we won't fail," she said, her voice steady with determination.

Marcel nodded, grateful for her unwavering support. In unison, they turned back to their work, the secure phone now silent but its implications lingering in the air.

Chapter 31

Chantelle braced herself as the sirens wailed in the distance, the sound cutting through the city's restless night. The emergency department was pandemonium incarnate—stretchers jammed into every available space, bloodied patients moaning or shouting, and the sharp, acrid smell of disinfectant mingling with sweat and fear.

She moved from one patient to the next with relentless efficiency, her years of training guiding her even as her mind wrestled with the broader implications of what she was seeing. Most of the cases bore the hallmarks of gang violence: gunshot wounds, knife slashes, and brutal injuries from close combat. But there were others—victims of overdoses or bizarre, sudden collapses with no apparent cause.

She approached a young man sprawled on a stretcher, his eyes glassy and his breathing shallow. His vital signs were erratic, and his skin had a sickly pallor. A nurse handed Chantelle the patient's chart, and she scanned it quickly.

"Drug overdose," the nurse murmured, her voice weary. "But his tox screen isn't consistent with what we usually see, and there is hardly a significant amount of alcohol in his blood."

Chantelle frowned, her mind flashing back to similar cases she'd seen in the past weeks. "Administer a saline drip and monitor his vitals," she instructed. She couldn't shake the sense that this was part of the same mysterious pattern she'd been investigating with her father and mother.

The doors to the ER banged open, and a group of paramedics rushed in, pushing a stretcher with a young woman barely clinging to life. The paramedic closest to Chantelle gave her a grim look. "Gunshot wound to the abdomen. She's part of one of the groups. There was a shootout downtown—three dead on the scene and more on the way."

Chantelle felt a chill run down her spine. The gang wars were escalating, and the city was teetering on the brink of collapse. She couldn't help but think of the larger implications. The mysterious deaths, the destabilisation of the drug trade, and the resulting violence were all interconnected. But why? And how?

As she worked to stabilise the new patient, her mind raced. What if the contamination was somehow triggering the violence? If the drug trade was faltering due to unexplained deaths among users, it would make sense that the cartels were scrambling to maintain control. The thought was chilling. What they had uncovered in the winery was no longer just a scientific anomaly—it was a catalyst for a societal collapse.

Later, as the confusion subsided and she found a moment to catch her breath, Chantelle sat down in the staff room, her head in her hands. Her phone buzzed, and she saw a message from her father.

We're heading into the city for a lead. We'll be careful. Let you know if anything happens.

Chantelle stared at the message, unease settling in her chest. If the city was this unstable, her family might be walking straight into danger. She had to get hold of them.

Chapter 32

Marcel and Genevieve stood at the edge of a dimly lit alley, the shadows cloaking them as they surveyed the scene. The faint sound of distant sirens underscored the eerie silence. Beside them, Chantelle adjusted her scarf, her eyes scanning the surroundings for any sign of trouble. She could not have left her parents on their own, happy that she managed to contact them and get picked up at the hospital.

"Are you sure about this, Marcel?" Genevieve asked, her voice low but tense. She clutched a notebook; its pages filled with observations and leads they had gathered.

Marcel nodded; his expression grim. "If the contamination is linked to the drugs circulating in the city, we need to trace it back to its source. The patterns suggest distribution hubs like this one. We have to investigate."

Chantelle remained quiet, but the tension in her posture was evident. She had agreed to accompany her parents out of a mix of professional curiosity and a fierce determination to protect them, but the unease she felt in the hospital had only deepened now that she was out in the field.

As they moved further into the alley, they came upon a scene that made them freeze. Several men stood clustered around a black SUV; their voices hushed but urgent. One of them, a burly figure with a scar running down his cheek, was gesturing angrily at the others.

"This batch is killing people," he snarled, his voice carrying in the stillness. "Our buyers are dropping dead, and the cops are breathing down our necks. If we don't fix this, we're finished."

Marcel motioned for Genevieve and Chantelle to stay back as he crept closer, straining to hear. The men were clearly part of a cartel, their anger fuelled by the mysterious deaths that had been plaguing the drug trade.

One of the other men spoke; his tone more measured. "We need to figure out what's causing it. If it's contamination, we might be able to spin it. Blame it on a rival gang or something."

Genevieve's grip on Marcel's arm tightened. "They're starting to suspect the truth," she whispered.

Before Marcel could respond, the men turned abruptly, their eyes scanning the alley. "Did you hear something?" one of them asked, reaching for his waistband where a gun was holstered.

Marcel gestured urgently for his family to retreat, but it was too late. One of the men spotted them, his face hardening. "Hey! Who's there?"
The group erupted into action. Two men drew weapons, while the others began closing the distance. Marcel's heart pounded as he pushed Chantelle and Genevieve behind a stack of crates. "Stay low," he hissed.

The men approached cautiously, their footsteps echoing in the narrow alley. Marcel reached into his coat and pulled out a small flashlight, clicking it on and off rapidly to disorient their pursuers. The sudden bursts of light bought them a few seconds, enough for the family to slip into a side passage.

They ran, their breaths ragged, as shouts and footsteps followed them. Chantelle's mind raced, her medical training providing no solace in a situation that was spiralling out of control. Genevieve clutched Marcel's hand, her scientific mind grappling with the surreal reality of being hunted by cartel members.

As they rounded a corner, they found themselves at a dead end. Marcel scanned the area desperately, spotting a fire escape ladder just within reach. "Up there!" he urged.

Chantelle climbed first, her movements swift despite the adrenaline coursing through her veins. Genevieve followed, and Marcel brought up the rear, pulling the ladder up just as their pursuers entered the alley.

From their perch on the rooftop, they watched as the men searched the area below, their curses filling the air. Marcel's chest heaved as he turned to his family. "We can't stay here. We need to get back to the chateau."

Genevieve nodded, her face pale but determined. "We need to regroup. This is bigger than we thought."

Descending from the rooftop was anything but easy. The worn tiles beneath their feet shifted with every step, threatening to betray their presence. Marcel led the way, his eyes scanning the narrow alley below for any sign of movement. Genevieve and Chantelle followed, their breaths shallow and quick as they clung to the walls for balance.

Every creak, every scrape seemed amplified in the tense silence, and the sound of footsteps echoing in the alley below sent their hearts racing. Marcel held up a hand, signalling them to stop as he peered over the edge of the building. The men were still searching, their voices sharp and angry, but they hadn't yet looked up.

Finally, they reached a fire escape that creaked ominously as they descended. Chantelle's foot slipped on the last rung, and Marcel reached out just in time to steady her. "Careful," he whispered, his voice barely audible.

Once on the ground, they moved quickly but cautiously, darting between shadows, always looking over their shoulders. The alley seemed endless, and the tension was suffocating. The moment they rounded the corner and spotted the Range Rover parked discreetly near a side street; a brief flicker of relief passed through them.

"Quickly," Marcel urged, unlocking the car with trembling hands.

As they piled into the vehicle; Chantelle cast one last glance behind them—and froze. "Papa," she whispered, her voice tight with fear. "I think they've seen us."

Marcel turned his head sharply, and his stomach sank. A black SUV idled at the end of the alley, its engine growling menacingly.

"They're following us," Chantelle said, her voice rising. Marcel didn't wait. The Range Rover roared to life, and he pulled out onto the narrow street, accelerating rapidly.

The SUV's headlights appeared in the rearview mirror, and Marcel tightened his grip on the steering wheel. Genevieve's voice was trembling but firm. "Marcel, get rid of them."

"I'm trying," he replied, his eyes darting between the road and the mirror.

The streets were a maze of narrow lanes and sharp turns, but the black SUV matched their every move. Chantelle kept glancing over her shoulder, her breath hitching each time the vehicle closed the gap. "They're not giving up!"

Marcel gritted his teeth, his mind racing. "Hold on," he said, veering sharply into a side street.

The tyres screeched as he navigated the twisting roads, the Range Rover's powerful engine straining as it picked up speed. He darted down alleyways and side streets, dodging delivery trucks and startled pedestrians. But no matter how many sharp turns he made, the SUV seemed to anticipate their every move.

Genevieve clutched the armrest, her knuckles white. "Marcel, they're still on us! We can't outrun them forever."

Suddenly, flashing lights appeared ahead—a cluster of police cars and an ambulance blocked part of the road, their blue and red lights cutting through the dark. Marcel's mind raced.
"That's it," he said, his voice firm. "Hang on."

Slowing just enough to blend in with the traffic, Marcel manoeuvred the Range Rover into the congestion surrounding the scene. Sirens wailed, and uniformed officers directed vehicles through the confusion. At the last moment, Marcel spotted a gap behind a parked police car and slid the Range Rover into it, effectively hiding in plain sight.

"Stay down," he instructed, his voice low.

Genevieve and Chantelle leaned forward; their heads barely visible over the dashboard. The black SUV sped past, its driver scanning the scene but not slowing.

They sat frozen, their breaths shallow, until the SUV disappeared into the distance. Then, as if on cue, they all exhaled deeply, their bodies sagging with relief.

"That was close," Marcel said, his voice shaky but tinged with determination. "Maybe too close."

Genevieve turned to him, her eyes wide with fear, her usually composed demeanour crumbling. "Marcel, this is scaring me," she said, her voice breaking. Tears streamed down her face as she struggled to contain her emotions.

Marcel reached out, his hand resting on hers. "I know," he said softly, his tone heavy with guilt. "I'm sorry. That was careless... and silly. I'll make sure this doesn't happen again."
Chantelle, still catching her breath, glanced between her parents. "We're in this together," she said, her voice

steady despite the lingering fear. "But we need to be smarter. This isn't just about the investigation anymore—it's about staying alive."

Marcel nodded, his jaw tightening. "You're right. From now on, we don't take any chances. We'll get back to the chateau, regroup, and figure out our next steps."

Genevieve wiped her tears, drawing a deep, shaky breath. "Marcel," she said, her voice softer now but no less resolute, "just promise me we'll get through this. Together."

Marcel met her gaze, his own resolve hardening. "I promise."

With the tension still observable but their determination renewed, Marcel started the engine, guiding the Range Rover carefully out of its hiding spot. The night was far from over, but for now, they had escaped the danger—and they were more united than ever.

Chantelle couldn't shake the realisation that their investigation had crossed a dangerous threshold. The stakes were no longer just scientific—they were life or death. And the cartel wasn't the only threat. The truth they were uncovering had the power to destabilise not just their city but the entire world.

Chapter 33

The soft glow of dawn filtered through the windows of Marcel's study, casting long shadows across the stacks of papers and the array of equipment spread across the room. Marcel and Genevieve had been working tirelessly through the night, piecing together the evidence that could exonerate them. The tension of the previous evening still lingered, but the urgency of their task overrode their exhaustion.

Earlier, they had conducted a painstaking inspection of the laboratory and its equipment. Every device, every tool, and every piece of furniture was scrutinised with meticulous care. Marcel and Genevieve worked silently, their movements methodical and precise, driven by the weight of their mission. Each drawer and shelf was emptied and sanitised; each instrument tested and calibrated.

As the hours stretched on, they extended their cleaning efforts to the walls, floors, and even the ceiling, ensuring that no surface was overlooked. The laboratory gleamed under the harsh fluorescent lights, the faint scent of disinfectant hanging in the air. They even tested their personal lab coats and clothing, determined to rule out any trace of contamination.

Then came the gloves.

Genevieve held up a pair of latex gloves, her expression unreadable. Marcel positioned the Geiger counter near them, his hand steady but his mind racing. The silence of the room was broken by a sudden *click-click-click*.

Their hearts stopped. The sound was faint but unmistakable, the Geiger counter registering a trace of radiation. Marcel and Genevieve exchanged a look of alarm, their breath catching as the clicks seemed to increase in tempo.

Marcel adjusted the counter, his hand trembling slightly. The clicks spiked briefly, then slowed, fading into near silence. Finally, the device recorded only the faintest trace of radioactivity—so minimal it was insignificant.

The room was still. They stared at each other, the relief palpable as they both exhaled deeply.

"Mon Dieu," Genevieve whispered, clutching the edge of the counter for support.

Marcel set the Geiger counter down, his shoulders relaxing slightly. "It's...nothing. The trace is so minute it's negligible. We're clear."

Marcel then added, "Besides, these were your inner gloves, Genevieve. Remember you always wore the heavy gloves Ivan gave us over them? I think the chances of them being contaminated are minimal."

For the first time in hours, they allowed themselves to breathe freely. The faint, transient reading had been enough to paralyse them with fear, but its insignificance rekindled a glimmer of hope.

Genevieve straightened, brushing a stray lock of hair from her face. Her exhaustion seemed momentarily forgotten. "If the gloves are clean...then so are we."

Marcel nodded; his expression resolute. "It's a start. A small step, but it means something. We just need to keep going."

That faint moment of terror had jolted them awake, and the relief that followed renewed their energy and focus. It wasn't proof, not yet—but it was a reason to believe.

The daunting experience left Marcel and Genevieve emotionally drained but resolute. As they closed the door to the freshly sanitised laboratory behind them, they decided to step outside and seek solace in the serenity of their vineyard. The late afternoon air was crisp and carried the earthy scent of fog-kissed vines. Hand in hand, they walked slowly between the rows, their breaths misting in the cool air.

The vineyard was a sanctuary, its beauty grounding them in a way that the sterile lab could not. The vibrant green leaves swayed gently in the breeze, and the occasional chirp of birds broke the silence. Each step seemed to ease the tension in their shoulders, and their clasped hands spoke volumes—offering comfort, unity, and strength.

"Every time I walk through here, I'm reminded why we do this," Genevieve said softly, her voice steady despite the whirlwind of thoughts running through her mind.

Marcel nodded, his eyes scanning the horizon. "This is our legacy. For us, for the children...we can't let it be tarnished. We won't."

Their walk ended at the terrace of the main house, where Genevieve served a pot of freshly brewed tea and a plate of her homemade cookies. The warmth of the tea, paired with the simple sweetness of the cookies, brought them a moment of comfort—a small reprieve in the midst of their relentless ordeal.

Feeling slightly renewed, they returned to Marcel's study. The stacks of papers and files awaited them, their task far from over. But now, with their hearts fortified by those few quiet moments, they dove back into the investigation with a renewed sense of purpose, ready to face whatever challenges lay ahead.

"Genevieve, hand me the timeline again," Marcel said, his voice sharp with focus. His fingers flew over his keyboard, cross-referencing shipments and laboratory records.

Genevieve pushed a stack of papers toward him, her eyes scanning another set of test results. "If the contamination didn't happen in our lab, it had to be introduced during processing or distribution. The question is—how?"

Marcel nodded, pulling up the detailed records of the deal with Giovanni Russo. They had licensed the preservative pills to his distribution company months before, with every batch thoroughly tested and certified as clean.

"Here," Marcel said, pointing to the shipping records. "The last tests were performed before the shipment left the chateau. No signs of radiation or anomalies."

Genevieve leaned over; her mind pensive. "Which means the contamination occurred afterwards. But that doesn't explain how radioactive material ended up in the supply chain."

Marcel stood; his gaze fixed on the board where they had mapped out their findings. "We need to consider every possibility. Could the contamination have been intentional? Or was it an accident?"

Before Genevieve could respond, the door opened, and Chantelle entered, holding her tablet. Her face was pale but determined. "I think I've found something," she said, crossing the room to join them. "I ran an analysis of the locations where the contaminated pills were distributed thanks to Henri's latest reports and cross-referenced them with radiation monitoring data. There's a pattern."

Genevieve sat up straighter. "A pattern?"

Chantelle nodded, pulling up a map on her tablet. Red dots marked the locations of contaminated shipments, and they clustered around industrial zones with known radiation risks. "These areas are hotspots for illicit activity—unregulated processing plants, illegal dumpsites. If Giovanni Russo's network used one of these facilities, it could explain the contamination."

Marcel's eyes narrowed as he studied the map. "Giovanni's reputation is as murky as it gets. If he's cutting costs by outsourcing to unregulated facilities, it's not just unethical—it's criminal. This could be our breakthrough."

As he spoke, Marcel glanced at Genevieve. He could feel the tension radiating from her, a tightness in her posture and a flicker of something unreadable in her eyes. He knew how much her breakthrough in preservation technology meant to her. It wasn't just a scientific achievement or a lucrative business venture—it was a deeply personal endeavour, a culmination of years of meticulous work and a reflection of her unwavering integrity.

For Genevieve, the deal with Russo had been a stepping stone, a means to bring her innovation to a wider audience. But it had never been about the money or the prestige. Marcel understood that her work was driven by a genuine desire to improve the quality of food and wine, to preserve the essence of nature's gifts, and possibly, to push the boundaries of what her research could contribute to medicine and beyond.

Now, all of that—the essence of her career and the principles she held dear—was under threat. And the thought that someone like Giovanni Russo, a man with questionable morals and dubious dealings, could tarnish her reputation filled Marcel with a simmering unease.

He clenched his jaw, his mind churning. This wasn't just about proving their innocence anymore. The stakes were higher. Genevieve's integrity and legacy were on the line, and the very reputation of their family was at risk. Marcel realised they were treading on dangerous territory.

For a moment, he felt the weight of the situation press heavily on his chest. They were caught between the devil and the deep blue sea. On one hand, they needed to ensure their safety and secure the protection promised to them by the president. On the other, revealing too much to the authorities too soon could expose them to even greater risks, especially if Russo caught wind of their findings before they had conclusive evidence to present.

Marcel exhaled sharply, forcing himself to stay focused. The discoveries they had made thus far—the contaminated shipments, the ties to Russo's network, the link to industrial zones riddled with radiation risks—were pieces of a puzzle. But the picture was far from complete. Every step they took needed to be calculated, every move strategic.

His gaze swept over Chantelle, who was diligently marking patterns on the map, her green eyes sharp with determination, and then back to Genevieve, whose lips were pressed into a thin line, her mind undoubtedly working through the implications of their findings.

For now, the only people he trusted implicitly were these two: his core team. The bond they shared as a family, combined with their collective expertise, was the strongest shield they had against the storm brewing around them. Until they had absolute, conclusive evidence to present to the president, the information and discoveries they had made needed to be contained within their tight-knit circle.

Marcel straightened; his voice steady but resolute. "We move carefully," he said, his tone leaving no room for argument. "For now, this stays between us. No one else—no officials, no authorities—until we have an airtight case. We can't afford any leaks or misunderstandings."

Genevieve nodded slowly, her tension easing slightly as she seemed to take comfort in his decisiveness. "Agreed. This is our responsibility, and we owe it to ourselves—and to the truth—to see it through."

Chantelle glanced up, her expression serious. "Understood, Papa. We'll be thorough. And we'll be careful."

Marcel placed a hand on Genevieve's shoulder, his grip firm but reassuring. "We'll get through this *ma chérie*."

Genevieve met his gaze, and in that moment, an unspoken agreement passed between them. This wasn't just about solving a mystery or clearing their names. It was about protecting everything they had built together—their work, their family, their legacy. And they would stop at nothing to see it done.

* * *

An hour later, the family gathered in Marcel's private lab, where they had set up a makeshift contamination-testing station. Genevieve carefully unpacked a sample of the preservative pills from the last shipment that had left their winery, handling the sealed container as though it were a volatile substance.

"These are from the clean batch we certified," she said, placing the container under the spectrometer. "If there's any contamination, it didn't happen here."
Marcel adjusted the machine, his movements precise. "Let's confirm it."

The spectrometer hummed to life, its readings appearing on the screen in real-time. The analysis showed no trace of radioactive isotopes, confirming their suspicions.

Genevieve let out a breath she hadn't realised she was holding. "It's clean. Just as we thought."

Marcel smiled, relief washing over him. "That clears our lab. Now let's test the samples Chantelle brought back from the hospital."

Chantelle stepped forward, placing a sealed vial on the counter. "These were confiscated from a patient who had a severe reaction. If these show contamination, we'll know it happened downstream."

The machine ran its analysis, and the results were starkly different. The contaminated pills showed alarming levels of radioisotopes, confirming that they had been tainted post-production.

Genevieve leaned against the counter, her hand covering her mouth. "It's true, then. The contamination didn't start with us."

Marcel nodded grimly. "This points directly to Giovanni Russo's operations. We need to trace the chain of custody for these shipments."

***

Genevieve leaned back in her chair, her arms crossed tightly as she stared at the data. The numbers and charts blurred before her eyes, overtaken by a flood of memories from the day she had met Giovanni Russo. She had been so convinced of his credibility back then. He had presented himself as a polished professional, with a sterling reputation in the wine and spirits industry. His marketing and distribution network was reputedly one of the finest in Europe, and his approach had seemed perfectly aligned with her vision.

Her mind drifted back to their meeting—Russo had been charming, exuding confidence and charisma, the kind of man who could effortlessly win over even the most sceptical of business partners. He had spoken passionately about expanding Genevieve's preservative technology to markets she had only dreamed of reaching. His assurances, coupled with glowing testimonials and an impeccable pitch, had left her with little reason to doubt him.

Now, as she stared at the undeniable evidence tying him to these horrifying events, fury bubbled within her. The scoundrel, she thought bitterly, had been hiding behind a meticulously constructed facade. She clenched her fists, her nails pressing into her palms as anger mixed with disgust. She had dealt with a gangster, a man who had likely used her innovation as a tool for his criminal empire.

Genevieve's jaw tightened as another thought struck her:

This could have ruined me. This could have destroyed my life, my work, my family.

The thought of the damage this man had caused—or could still cause—filled her with a simmering rage that she rarely allowed herself to feel. For a moment, fear threatened to creep in, but she pushed it aside.

Instead, she clung to the one lifeline she had: her belief in her own integrity. The more she reflected on the chain of events, the more convinced she became that her hands were clean. She had done everything aboveboard, conducted rigorous testing, and ensured the highest standards. The contamination had occurred after the product had left her control—she was sure of it.

And if that was the case, then the blame lay squarely at Giovanni Russo's feet.

Her anger sharpened into determination. She wasn't just going to prove her innocence—she was going to expose him for what he truly was. The thought of him being brought to justice, of his operations being dismantled, gave her a sense of purpose that burned away her lingering doubts.

Genevieve sat up straighter, her green eyes flashing with resolve. "Marcel," she said, her voice steady but laced with steel, "we're going to prove it. Every last detail. We'll trace every shipment, and uncover every link. And when we do, Giovanni Russo will pay for what he's done."

Marcel met her gaze, nodding in agreement. "We will," he said simply, his voice carrying the same quiet intensity.

Chantelle, who had been poring over the medical data, looked up and added, "And I'll make sure the hospitals have the evidence they need to connect the deaths to his shipments. Once we have all the pieces, there will be nowhere for him to hide."

Genevieve took a deep breath, steadying herself. She couldn't let her anger cloud her judgment. The task ahead required precision, strategy, and collaboration. She glanced at her husband and daughter, their faces set with determination. They were in this together, and together, they would prevail.

In that moment, Genevieve's resolve crystallised into an unshakable belief: this wasn't just about clearing her name. This was about justice, about protecting her family and ensuring that her life's work wasn't tainted by the actions of a criminal.

Russo had underestimated her. That much she was sure of. But he was about to learn that the Dupont family wasn't so easily defeated.

* * *

As night fell, the family regrouped in the chateau's sitting room. The tension had eased slightly, replaced by a sense of determination.

"We have the evidence to clear our names," Marcel said, his voice firm. "Now we need to ensure that Giovanni Russo is held accountable."

Genevieve nodded, her expression resolute. "Absolutely! But again, we must tread carefully. If we expose this without proper safeguards, we risk putting ourselves—and the evidence—in danger."

Chantelle spoke up, her tone measured. "We need to present this to the authorities. Hopefully, they see to it that preventative measures are put in place so that this doesn't occur again."

Marcel looked at his daughter with pride. "You're right. We'll present our investigation with results, solid proof, and recommendations."

Genevieve placed a hand on Marcel's shoulder. "Like the old days *mon cher*. Whatever comes next, we'll face it together, just like the old days."

* * *

The next morning, Marcel gathered the family in the spacious kitchen of the chateau. The early sunlight filtered through the tall windows, casting warm streaks over the wooden table where Genevieve, Chantelle, and Jean-Pierre sat, waiting expectantly.

Marcel stood at the head of the table, his presence commanding yet unusually vulnerable.

"I've thought about this all night," he began, his voice steady but carrying the weight of his decision. "We cannot remain silent. But we will not act recklessly either. There's a way to address this that minimises harm while ensuring the truth comes to light."

Genevieve reached for his hand, her expression supportive yet apprehensive. "What do you propose, Marcel?"

"We need proof, physical evidence—irrefutable evidence that the contamination occurred after the deal with Giovanni Russo. If we can present to the president a clear timeline with this evidence, and trace the radioactive material to his distribution network; we can clear our name while ensuring the issue is addressed responsibly."

Jean-Pierre nodded, his hazel eyes narrowing in thought. "It's risky, but it's the right approach. If we can find the source, we might even help stop this before it escalates further."

Chantelle chimed in, her voice firm. "I'll continue monitoring the cases at the hospital and have the data ready to share with the authorities. If we can tie the deaths to specific batches of contaminated pills, it might lead us to the origin and assist them."

Genevieve looked thoughtful, her scientific mind already piecing together a plan. "We still have records of the batches we produced. If we can secure samples from Russo's distribution chain linked to these batches, we can confirm that the contamination happened post-production."

As the family spoke, Marcel felt the weight on his shoulders again and leaned against the table's edge, his hands gripping its surface. Each family member's input was valid and worthy, but somehow, he suddenly felt immense pressure on him to prove his innocence. They had proved it in their laboratory but was this enough? The strain on his face was evident, his usual air of composure slipping.

"This is bigger than us," he muttered, almost to himself. "I've dedicated my life to science, to understanding the universe's complexities, yet here I am, unable to ensure my family's safety. What if this spirals out of control? What if—"

Jean-Pierre interrupted, stepping closer to his father. "Papa, stop." His voice was calm but firm, a rare edge of authority cutting through the tension. "You've always told me that fear and doubt are distractions from the problem. You taught me to look at facts, to stay grounded, and to trust the process. Why would this be any different?"

Marcel looked up, meeting his son's steady gaze. The intensity in Jean-Pierre's hazel eyes mirrored his own, a reflection of the man he had raised. "This isn't just about solving a scientific puzzle, Jean-Pierre. It's about protecting all of you. I can't—"

"You *are* protecting us," Jean-Pierre said, his voice unwavering. "Every step you've taken, every decision you've made, has been to shield this family and find the truth. You've always shown me that we face challenges head-on, no matter how daunting. And we're not in this alone."

Genevieve stepped closer, placing a hand on Marcel's arm. "Jean-Pierre's right. You've always led with courage, Marcel, and we're here to support you. We'll get through this together."

Chantelle, who had been quietly observing, added softly, "You've been the backbone of this family for so long, Papa. Let us share the weight. That's what families do."

Marcel's grip on the table loosened, his shoulders relaxing slightly as the words settled over him. He glanced at Jean-Pierre, a flicker of pride breaking through the worry.

"You've grown into a remarkable man," he said quietly. "I see so much of your mother's strength and your own quiet resolve. Thank you."

Jean-Pierre gave a small, reassuring smile. "We're Duponts, Papa. We don't back down from challenges. And you're not alone in this."

The tension in the room eased, replaced by a renewed sense of determination. Marcel straightened, his expression softening as he looked around at his family.

"You're right. This isn't just my fight—it's ours. Together, we'll find the evidence we need and put this nightmare behind us."

"Exactly," Jean-Pierre said, clapping his father lightly on the shoulder. "Now, let's focus. Where were we?"

Marcel placed his hands on the table again, gaining strength as he leaned toward his family. "This will require absolute precision and irrefutable evidence. We'll be walking a tightrope—balancing transparency with self-preservation. But if we work together, package the facts and evidence we have gathered in an irrefutable timeline" he paused, letting the break in speech capture attention. He continued, "I believe we can do it."

Genevieve met his gaze, her confidence returning. "Then let's start. I want to finalise this."

* * *

As the family finalised their plans, Marcel allowed himself a moment of quiet reflection. The events of the past weeks had tested them in ways he could never have anticipated, but they had emerged stronger, united by their shared purpose.

He felt like the truth was out, even though only to them, and he knew that they needed solid proof. While the road ahead was still uncertain, Marcel knew one thing for sure: the Duponts would not be defined by fear or suspicion.

They would be defined by their perseverance, their resilience, their integrity, and their unwavering commitment to justice.

Chapter 34

Genevieve moved through the rows of her herb garden, a basket in one hand as she plucked sprigs of thyme and rosemary. The sun was setting, casting long shadows across the chateau grounds, and a faint breeze carried the crisp, earthy scent of autumn leaves. Her fingers grazed over the soft leaves of basil, her mind momentarily at ease as she considered the menu for the evening—something hearty and grounding, a celebration of their recent breakthrough and resolve.

As she reached for a cluster of fresh parsley, a glint of black at the edge of the driveway caught her eye. Straightening, she squinted toward the road. A sleek, black SUV sat idle at the end of the long, gravel path leading to their home. Its windows were tinted, offering no hint of its occupants.

Genevieve's heart quickened. She set the basket down, wiping her hands on her apron, and took a step forward, her breath catching as she noticed the faint plume of exhaust from the idling vehicle. It didn't belong to anyone she recognised—friends and delivery vehicles rarely lingered at such a distance.

Moving cautiously, she circled toward the edge of the garden to get a better view. As she crept closer, her pulse drummed in her ears. A sudden movement in the vineyard drew her attention, and relief flooded her as she spotted Jean-Pierre, his broad figure silhouetted against the golden vines.

"Jean-Pierre!" she called out, her voice sharper than she intended.

Her son turned, concern flashing in his hazel eyes as he set down the pruning shears and jogged toward her.

"What is it, *Maman*?" he asked, his tone calm but alert. Genevieve grabbed his arm, her grip firm, and pulled him toward the house. "There's a car at the end of the driveway," she said, her voice trembling. "I don't like it. It's been sitting there, just watching. Come, let's go inside. Now."

Jean-Pierre frowned, glancing over his shoulder toward the driveway. "A car? Are you sure it's not someone lost or waiting for directions?"

"I know what I saw," Genevieve snapped, her fear overriding her usual composure. "Please, Jean-Pierre, inside!"

As they approached the house, Genevieve's voice carried through the open kitchen window. "Marcel!" she called out, her tone shrill.

Marcel, who had been preparing a pot of coffee, turned sharply at the sound of her voice. His hazel eyes met hers as she rushed into the kitchen, still clutching Jean-Pierre's arm.

"What's wrong?" Marcel asked, his voice steady but laced with concern.

Genevieve released Jean-Pierre and wrung her hands, her words tumbling out in a frantic stream. "There's a car—a black SUV—at the end of the driveway. It's just sitting there, Marcel. Who are they? Why are they here?

What do they want?" Her voice cracked, and she gripped the edge of the counter as if to steady herself. "Marcel, I'm starting to panic. I'm scared, Marcel."

From the adjacent room, Chantelle appeared, drawn by her mother's panic. Her green eyes darted between her parents, her brow channelled with concern. "*Maman*, what's going on?" she asked, her voice soft but firm.

Genevieve turned to her daughter, her fear now spilling over. "Chantelle, there's a car—a suspicious car! I know something's wrong. It's the black SUV. The one that followed us the other night. They've found us. I don't like it. What if they've come for us? What if they know?"

Jean-Pierre, his face taut with concern, stepped forward.

"Let me go take a look," he said, his voice measured.

"No!" Genevieve said sharply, grabbing his arm again. "We stay together. We don't know who they are or what they want."

Marcel moved to her side, placing a reassuring hand on her shoulder. "Genevieve, calm yourself," he said, his voice low and steady. "We don't know anything yet. Panicking won't help."

"How can you be so calm?" Genevieve snapped, her fear making her voice rise. "What if they're here to hurt us? Or to silence us? I don't like this, Marcel"

Marcel met her gaze, his expression firm. "Because we need to think clearly. Fear clouds judgment. Let's assess the situation rationally."

Chantelle stepped closer to her mother, wrapping an arm around her shoulders. "*Maman*, *Papa*'s right. We're stronger together, and we'll figure this out. But first, we need to breathe."

Genevieve took a shaky breath, her fingers trembling as she reached for the glass of water Chantelle handed her.

Jean-Pierre crossed his arms, his jaw tight. "If they're watching us, it's because they know we've uncovered something. That makes us a threat—but it also means they're scared of what we might do."

Marcel nodded, his mind already racing through possibilities. "Exactly. They're trying to intimidate us. But we have the truth on our side, and we have a fair amount of proof. That gives us the upper hand."
Genevieve looked at him, her eyes wide and pleading. "But what if it's not enough? What if they don't care about proof?"

Marcel took her hands in his, his touch steady and grounding. "Listen to me, Genevieve. We've come too far to back down now. We'll remain calm and vigilant."

Chantelle stepped forward, her voice clear and resolute. "We can't let fear paralyse us. We've always faced challenges as a family, and this is no different. We'll stick together through this one also."

Jean-Pierre nodded in agreement. "I'll secure the house. If they're still there in the morning, we can consider our next move. But for tonight, we stay alert and stay inside."

Marcel turned to his son, pride flickering in his eyes. "Good. Let's make sure all doors and windows are locked. No one leaves the house until we know what we're dealing with."
Genevieve exhaled slowly, some of the tension leaving her shoulders. "Okay," she said quietly. "We stay together. We face this together."

As the family moved through the house, checking locks and drawing curtains, a sense of unity settled over them. The fear that had threatened to unravel them was now channelled into purposeful action.

Later, as they gathered in the living room, Marcel laid out his plan, his voice calm but firm. "First thing tomorrow, I'll contact the authorities and tell them that we will be ready soon to report back to the President. We have come too far to let this beat us when all we need is that final piece of the jigsaw. I will provide them with our findings once we have retrieved that final and irrefutable piece of proof to conclude our report. We'll make sure they understand the caution and discretion that is required at this final stage. For now, we rest. We need clear minds for what's ahead."

Genevieve leaned into Marcel, her head resting on his shoulder. "You're right," she murmured. "We've come too far to let fear win."

Jean-Pierre sat nearby, his gaze thoughtful. "We'll protect what matters—our family, our home, and the truth."

Chantelle smiled faintly, her hand resting on her mother's. "We've always been resilient. This won't be any different."

As the night deepened and the family settled in for an uneasy rest, the SUV at the end of the driveway remained a silent sentinel, its purpose unknown but its presence undeniable.

But within the walls of the chateau, a quiet resolve took root—a determination to face whatever lay ahead, together.

Chapter 35

By afternoon, the Dupont family was hard at work. The SUV had gone, bringing desperate and needed sighs of relief to all of them. Marcel and Genevieve combed through production records in the winery's office, their meticulous notes piecing together the timeline of the deal with Russo. Jean-Pierre coordinated with trusted contacts in the wine industry, seeking any whispers about irregularities in Russo's supply chain.

Chantelle, meanwhile, worked from her station at the hospital. Between shifts, she compiled data on the patients affected by the mysterious deaths, cross-referencing their cases with any known drug batches. Each discovery added another thread to the intricate web they were weaving.

They had a plan, and they were piecing the timeline together from start to end, piece by piece, and fact by fact.

Hours later, Marcel and Genevieve struck another piece of gold. In the back of her filing cabinet, she dug out the part of the contract detailing the precise terms of their deal with Russo. It included a stipulation requiring independent testing of the preservative pills before shipment—a precaution Genevieve had insisted on.

"Look at this," Genevieve said, holding up the document. "The final test results show no trace of radioactive contamination. That means the product was clean when it left our hands."

Marcel exhaled, a glimmer of relief breaking through his tension. "This is exactly what we needed. It will fit perfectly into that part of the timeline. But we still need more than paperwork to convince anyone. We need more physical evidence."

Genevieve nodded. "Then we'll have to obtain samples from Russo's batches that tie in with the batch number and we can compare them to our originals and prove the contamination occurred later. That will strengthen the case and support the paper work."

Marcel frowned, his thoughts turning to logistics. "Getting access to Russo's product won't be easy. We can't approach him directly without raising suspicion."

Jean-Pierre stepped into the room, his expression resolute. "Leave that to me. I have a contact who works in distribution—someone who might be willing to help us under the radar."

Marcel hesitated. "This could be dangerous, Jean-Pierre."

Jean-Pierre's eyes were unwavering. "We don't have a choice, *Papa*. I'll be careful."

* * *

That evening, Jean-Pierre met with his contact, a middle-aged man named Victor who had worked in the wine distribution business for decades. They sat in a quiet corner of a small café, speaking in hushed tones.

"I need your help," Jean-Pierre said, sliding a folded sheet of paper across the table. It detailed the specific batch numbers associated with the contamination. "These batches were distributed by certain, possibly questionable networks. I need samples—untouched, if possible."

Victor frowned, his expression guarded. "You're asking me to put my neck on the line, Jean-Pierre. If these 'questionable networks' find out…"

"I understand the risk," Jean-Pierre said. "But this goes beyond business. We're looking into irregularities that could have serious consequences. If there's anything unusual in the supply chain—anything at all—it's crucial we uncover it. Your insights could make all the difference."

Victor sighed, glancing around the café before nodding reluctantly. "I'll see what I can do. But if anyone asks, this conversation never happened."

Jean-Pierre clasped his hand. "Thank you."

* * *

A week later, Victor delivered. The Dupont family gathered in the winery's lab as Genevieve carefully unpacked the sealed vials he had provided. Each was labelled with a batch number corresponding to the shipments they had sent to Russo.

"Let's hope this gives us the answers we need," Genevieve murmured as she began testing the samples.

"It will make our previous tests conclusive and add weight as irrefutable evidence." She added with a sense of hope.

Marcel and Jean-Pierre watched anxiously as she worked, Chantelle joining them via video call from the hospital.

Hours passed as Genevieve conducted a series of analyses, her focus unwavering. Finally, she straightened, holding a printout of the test results.

"It's there," she said, her voice trembling with a mix of triumph and relief. "The radioactive contamination is present—but only in the samples from Russo's batches. Our original preservative was clean."

Marcel let out a long breath, his shoulders sagging with relief. "That's it. It's not us, and that's conclusive."

Chantelle's voice crackled over the speaker. "This is huge. If you're telling me that we can tie this to Russo's operations, then we have shifted the focus of the investigation away from the winery."

Genevieve nodded, her expression hardening. "Correct, and we can ensure the contamination is stopped at its source."

Marcel placed a hand on her shoulder. "You've done it, Genevieve. We've done it. But this is just the beginning. Now we need to decide how to present this information—to the President and to how many other people."

As the family gathered around the lab table, the weight of the evidence settled over them. The truth was no longer a burden to bear alone—it was a weapon they could wield to protect their legacy and prevent further loss of life.

Marcel would present it diligently and together, they would see it through.

Chapter 36

The Duponts stood at the entrance of the Swiss Federal Palace, their expressions a mixture of determination and apprehension. Marcel carried a leather-bound folder containing their findings, the culmination of weeks of sleepless nights and meticulous research. Chantelle and Jean-Pierre flanked him, while Genevieve stood close, her presence a steadying force.

Inside, they were led to a grand conference room where the President of Switzerland, Philippe Morel, awaited them. The tall, silver-haired leader rose from his seat, extending his hand to Marcel. His calm demeanour carried an air of gravitas, though his piercing blue eyes betrayed the weight of the crisis they were here to address.

"Professor Dupont," President Morel said warmly, shaking Marcel's hand firmly. "I knew I could count on you. Your reputation precedes you, and your dedication to the truth is why I reached out."

Marcel inclined his head. "Thank you, Mr. President. I hope what we've uncovered will help address this crisis."

The President gestured for them to sit. "Let's hear what you've found."

Marcel opened the folder, revealing a series of documents and test results. Genevieve leaned forward, helping him arrange the pages as he began.

Marcel cleared his throat, glancing at Genevieve for a moment before addressing the president with measured calm.

"Our research confirms that the catalyst for the deadly reaction was a radioactive isotope," he began, his voice steady yet laced with gravity. "This isotope was introduced into liquor as an additive, delivered through preservation tablets intended to extend shelf life. The combination of chemical elements found in drugs, alcohol, and human blood, when exposed to this radioactive contamination, formed a lethal concoction.

My report meticulously documents the interaction of these molecular compounds with radioactive isotopes, detailing how their reactions spiral into toxicity."

He paused, gauging the president's reaction before continuing. "I must also disclose the origins of the preservative tablets in question. These tablets were developed as part of my wife Genevieve's research—a groundbreaking innovation in food and beverage preservation. However, she licensed their production and distribution to Giovanni Russo, believing him to be a reputable businessman."

The president seemed shocked at first, somewhat taken aback. He sat, not knowing what to say, and then his expression shifted subtly, his brows furrowing at the mention of Russo. His eyes sharpened, betraying a mixture of concern and intrigue, though he remained silent, seemingly trying to take it all in. He shifted in his seat and remained silent, allowing Marcel to proceed.

Marcel pressed on, his tone resolute. "We were shocked and also taken aback," he said, pausing to look at the president, "but we've since uncovered irrefutable proof that the contamination occurred after the pills left our facility. Every batch produced under our supervision was rigorously tested and confirmed free of any impurities. The contamination, as our findings indicate, was introduced post-production—specifically during the distribution phase within Russo's network."

The weight of the evidence hung in the air as Marcel concluded this critical revelation. He stood firm, his gaze unwavering as he awaited the president's response, ready to defend their integrity and demonstrate that the Dupont family had no hand in the horrors unleashed by this crisis.

Genevieve added, "The radioactive material found in the affected batches does not match anything present in our winery or our manufacturing process. We suspect it was introduced deliberately—though we cannot yet determine the motive."

Chantelle spoke next, her voice steady. "The autopsies and hospital data confirm a direct link between the contaminated batches and the deaths. We've cross-referenced patient records with distribution timelines. There's a clear pattern."

President Morel leaned back in his chair, his expression thoughtful as he absorbed the information. Finally, he spoke.

"This is extraordinary work. You've not only protected your family's name—dare I say an unexpected revelation—but also given us the key to understanding and stopping this crisis."

Marcel hesitated before responding. "Mr. President, we wanted to act responsibly, but we also feared the consequences of coming forward. The world is already on edge. Any misstep could lead to widespread panic— or worse."

The president nodded gravely.

"And you were right to be cautious. But rest assured, Professor Dupont, you and your family have my full support. I will personally ensure your safety."

He rose, walking to the window overlooking the capital. "This is a matter of international significance. I will inform Interpol immediately and share your findings with their task force. We'll coordinate with them to investigate Russo's network and trace the contamination to its source."

Turning back to face them, his expression softened. "You've done Switzerland—and the world—a great service. Your actions will save lives, and history will remember that."

Marcel felt a surge of relief, though the weight of responsibility still lingered. "Thank you, Mr. President. We trust your judgment on how to proceed."

President Morel extended his hand once more. "You trusted me to guide this process, and I trusted you to deliver the truth. Together, we'll see this through."

As they left the Federal Palace, the Dupont family felt a renewed sense of purpose. The truth was now in capable hands, and the path forward, though uncertain, was one they would no longer walk alone.

Chapter 37

The world was changing, and for once, the headlines were not filled with despair. Across the globe, a seismic shift was taking place, leaving both havoc and unexpected calm in its wake. News anchors spoke in urgent tones, yet their words carried an air of cautious optimism.

"This is Sarah Meyers reporting live from Geneva," began the poised news anchor on one of Switzerland's leading news channels. Her image flickered on the television screen in the Dupont household, her voice cutting through the quiet living room.

"We're witnessing what experts are calling an unprecedented collapse of the global drug trade. In the past two weeks alone, Interpol and law enforcement agencies worldwide have dismantled over thirty major cartel networks. Supply chains are in disarray, and drug-related violence has plummeted."

The camera cut to footage of armed raids on cartel hideouts, dramatic takedowns of notorious drug lords, and scenes of burning stockpiles of confiscated drugs. The images were stark, almost surreal. For decades, these cartels had operated with near-impunity, their influence so entrenched that many had believed dismantling them was a futile effort. Now, they were crumbling.

"Authorities attribute this rapid disintegration to an unexplained phenomenon," Meyers continued. "Thousands of gang members, dealers, and users have died mysteriously, leaving entire criminal networks vulnerable. This disruption has allowed law enforcement to strike where it once seemed impossible."

Jean-Pierre, seated in a leather armchair with his hazel eyes fixed on the screen, leaned forward. "It's unbelievable," he murmured. "It's like the entire system is eating itself alive."

Marcel, standing by the window with a glass of wine in hand, remained silent, his expression contemplative. He had been following the news closely, each update reinforcing what he already knew. The mysterious deaths that began in a sense with their winery's preservative pills had unravelled the criminal underworld in ways no one could have anticipated. Marcel and Genevieve's discovery of the radioactive contamination and its interaction with drugs had triggered a global chain reaction that neither had foreseen nor intended. Yet here they were, witnessing a profound transformation.

The news shifted to a montage of scenes from around the world: bustling streets in Mexico City, now quieter and devoid of their usual mayhem; the favelas of Rio de Janeiro, where graffiti calling for peace had replaced gang insignias; and neighbourhoods in Chicago where families walked freely without fear of crossfire.

Governments, too, were adapting. The Swiss president had addressed the nation earlier that week, lauding the "remarkable efforts of science and law enforcement" in combating the crisis. Marcel and his team were not present during that meeting but stood together and watched as the president commended their findings. While he had assured them of safety and discretion, Marcel couldn't shake the weight of their unintentional role in this upheaval.

At Chantelle's hospital, the changes were observable. The emergency ward, once overrun with drug overdoses, gang-related injuries, and the toll of addiction, was unusually quiet. Walking through the hospital corridors that afternoon, Chantelle was struck by the calm. A nurse passing by with a clipboard gave her a knowing smile.

"Feels strange, doesn't it?" she said. "It's like the city just... stopped hurting."

Chantelle nodded. "It's a good kind of strange," she replied, though her thoughts were far from settled. The unexplained deaths that had emptied the streets of gang members and dealers had also claimed the lives of ordinary people caught in the crossfire of addiction. Despite the visible improvements, Chantelle couldn't ignore the shadow that lingered over these events.

Later, in the break room, Chantelle joined a group of doctors discussing the dramatic drop in drug-related cases.

"Emergency intakes are down by nearly forty percent this month," one of her colleagues remarked. "Whatever's happening out there, it's working."

"Working, sure," another doctor interjected, stirring his coffee absently. "But at what cost? Hundreds, maybe thousands of unexplained deaths. It's hard to celebrate when we don't even know what we're dealing with."

Chantelle kept her thoughts to herself, though her mind raced. She knew more than she could ever share—not just about the mysterious deaths but about her parents' involvement. And while the scientist in her marvelled at the unintended consequences of their discovery, the doctor in her struggled with the ethical implications.

The world was adjusting, slowly but surely. In cities and towns where drug-related violence had once dictated daily life, there was an unfamiliar stillness. Schools reported higher attendance rates as fewer children were pulled into the disruption of gang life. Local businesses flourished in neighbourhoods where crime had once deterred customers.

Governments celebrated the decline in crime rates, attributing the success to enhanced policing and international cooperation. Yet in private, leaders grappled with the reality: they had been given a gift, but its origins were shrouded in secrecy. Scientists and investigators were still piecing together the puzzle of what had triggered the mysterious deaths, while conspiracy theories flourished among the public. Some claimed divine intervention; others speculated about a secret government weapon.

Genevieve, ever the optimist, saw the changes through a different lens. That evening, as she stood in the garden harvesting rosemary for supper, she reflected on how nature always found a way to heal itself. In her eyes, the world was undergoing a form of ecological and social balance, correcting the damage caused by decades of unchecked greed and violence.

"It's like pruning a vine," she told Marcel later that night. "Painful in the moment, but necessary for new growth."

* * *

At the end of the day, the Dupont family gathered in the sitting room, the soft crackle of the fireplace filling the silence. Chantelle, still in her hospital scrubs, sipped tea as she recounted the day's events.

"It's quieter now," she said, her voice contemplative. "Less confusion in the ER. Fewer drug cases. Even the nurses are starting to relax."

Jean-Pierre, seated opposite her, nodded.

"It's the same at the winery. Local vendors have been saying the same thing—less crime, more business. People seem... lighter, like they're not looking over their shoulders anymore."

Marcel listened intently, his fingers steepled as he processed their words. "The world is changing faster than anyone anticipated," he said finally. "But we can't let ourselves be lulled into thinking it's over. There are still pieces of this puzzle we don't understand."

Genevieve reached for his hand, her touch grounding him. "You're right, Marcel. But look at what's happening. The world is healing, in its own way. We can't ignore the good that's come from this."

Chantelle hesitated, her green eyes searching her father's face. "Do you think it'll last?" she asked softly. "This... peace?"

Marcel's expression softened as he regarded his daughter. "I hope so," he said. "But lasting peace requires more than the absence of violence. It requires understanding, compassion, and a commitment to do better." For a second Marcel thought of Ivan.

Jean-Pierre raised his glass in a quiet toast. "To doing better," he said.

The family clinked glasses, their shared silence heavy with unspoken thoughts. The crisis was far from over, but for the first time in months, there was a glimmer of hope—a sense that the world, scarred as it was, might yet find its way to a better future.

Chapter 38

The morning sun crept over the jagged peaks of the Swiss Alps, casting a glow of warmth on the freshly powdered slopes. The air was crisp, the kind of chill that made cheeks flush and breath visible in soft puffs.

The Dupont family had risen early, eager to spend the day on the mountain. It was a rare occasion to leave behind the weight of recent events and immerse themselves in something purely joyful.

Marcel led the way, his form sleek and precise as he cut through the snow with effortless elegance. Decades of skiing had honed his technique into something almost artistic. Behind him, Genevieve followed, her movements fluid and graceful, her scarf trailing like a banner as she swayed from turn to turn. The couple moved as if in a synchronized dance, their paths weaving together in the soft powder.

Farther up the slope, Jean-Pierre and Chantelle stood side by side, their skis pointed downhill as they eyed each other with competitive grins.

"You ready for this?" Jean-Pierre asked, adjusting his goggles with a flourish. His hazel eyes sparkled with mischief.

"Always," Chantelle shot back, her green eyes narrowing in mock defiance. "But let's be clear, Jean-Pierre: it's not about speed. It's about grace."

"Grace doesn't win races," he retorted, already pushing off with a burst of energy.

Chantelle laughed, launching herself after him. The two raced side by side, carving sharp turns and kicking up clouds of snow as they flew down the slope. Chantelle's athletic build gave her a natural edge in agility, while Jean-Pierre relied on sheer power to maintain his lead. The wind whipped against their faces, carrying their laughter as they traded mock insults.

"Is that the best you can do?" Chantelle called, her voice lilting with playful challenge as she overtook him on a particularly tight turn.

Jean-Pierre grinned, digging his edges into the snow to catch up. "Careful, little sister, or I might start taking it easy on you."

Marcel had paused at the edge of the slope, his skis crunching softly against the snow. Below him, Chantelle's laughter echoed as she chased Jean-Pierre, their playful rivalry leaving trails in the powdery white expanse.

Genevieve glided effortlessly, her figure a vision of grace against the backdrop of towering pines. For a moment, Marcel stood still, letting the crisp mountain air fill his lungs. This was his haven—his family, his anchor amidst the disorderliness of the world.

Chantelle and Jean-Pierre reached the base of the slope nearly at the same time, collapsing in a heap of laughter and catching their breath. Chantelle pulled off her goggles, her dark hair spilling loose around her face, and looked up to see her parents descending the slope with the kind of practised ease that came from years of experience.

"They make it look too easy," Jean-Pierre said, shaking his head in mock admiration.

Chantelle followed his gaze, watching as their parents glided effortlessly down the mountainside. Marcel led the way, his movements precise and deliberate, carving through the snow with a grace that belied his analytical mind. Skiing was an escape for him, a rare opportunity to let go of control and simply feel. As he leaned into each turn, the sharp, cold air stung his face, but it carried with it a clarity he cherished. For a moment, the demands of the world and the weight of his scientific endeavours melted away, leaving only the pure, exhilarating rhythm of the descent.

Genevieve followed close behind, her style equally elegant but with a touch of playful spontaneity. She moved with the fluidity of someone who saw beauty in every motion, her scarf trailing behind her like a ribbon in the wind. For her, skiing was more than a sport—it was a dance with nature. Each swoop and glide was a connection to the mountain, a reminder of the simplicity and joy that life could offer amidst its complexities. She let out a small whoop of delight as she caught a pocket of fresh powder, her laughter carrying down the slope like music.

At the base, Jean-Pierre adjusted his goggles, squinting up at the brilliant sunlit expanse. He loved these moments when his family was together, free from the vineyard's responsibilities or the shadows of the world's confusion. Skiing was his reset button, a chance to channel his energy into something physical, to compete with his sister and tease her when he inevitably won. Though he would never admit it aloud, he admired her tenacity, the way she pushed herself even in play.

Chantelle, catching her breath, leaned back in the snow, letting her legs rest for a moment. The crisp mountain air filled her lungs, invigorating her after long nights in the hospital. Here, on the slopes, she felt untethered from the demands of her medical studies and the weight of the cases she had carried. Her laughter came easily, a sound that echoed her freedom. She looked at Jean-Pierre and stuck out her tongue playfully.

 "If you'd been just a little faster, maybe you could've beaten me this time."

"Oh, please," Jean-Pierre replied, brushing snow from his jacket. "If skiing were about speed alone, I'd win every time. You just get lucky."

"It's not about speed," Chantelle shot back, grinning as she threw a handful of snow at him. "It's about grace."

Before Jean-Pierre could retort, Marcel and Genevieve reached them, their skis cutting smoothly to a stop. Marcel adjusted his hat, his breath visible in the icy air. "Looks like you two are ready for another run," he said, noting their rosy cheeks and competitive banter.

Genevieve took in the scene with a contented smile, the warmth of family filling her heart even in the chill of the mountain. "Or," she suggested, glancing toward the tree-lined trail ahead, "we could take the mountain road through the forest."

Jean-Pierre raised an eyebrow, his competitive streak momentarily subdued by curiosity. "You mean the scenic route?"

"Yes," Genevieve replied, her voice tinged with enthusiasm. "It's beautiful this time of year. The trees, the snow, the quiet—it's magical."

Chantelle nodded in agreement, already imagining the serene path winding through the woods. "Let's do it."

Marcel exchanged a knowing glance with Genevieve. "All right," he said, his tone light but teasing. "But don't get too distracted by the scenery. We're skiing, not mushroom picking."

Genevieve rolled her eyes with a laugh. "It's so peaceful through there but don't worry, Marcel. I'll keep up."

Jean-Pierre groaned in mock protest. "Peaceful? Are we skiing or going for a stroll?"

"Grace, Jean-Pierre," Chantelle teased, nudging him playfully. "It's about grace."
"Let's see how graceful you are dodging trees," he quipped, earning a laugh from his sister.

Together, the family adjusted their gear and set off toward the forested path, the laughter and camaraderie of the slopes lingering in their smiles.

They reached the winding mountain road as the forest enveloped them in a serene embrace. The towering pines, their branches heavy with snow, formed a natural cathedral, and the quiet crunch of skis against snow was the only sound.

Genevieve couldn't help but slow her pace, her gaze wandering to the sunlight filtering through the trees, casting dappled patterns on the pristine snow. The forest was alive with subtle sounds: the distant call of a bird, the creak of branches under the weight of snow, and the soft whoosh of her family's skis ahead of her.

"Stop dawdling, Genevieve," Marcel called back, his voice tinged with playful impatience. "We're not picking mushrooms."

Genevieve laughed, her breath visible in the cold air.

"Can't a woman appreciate the beauty of nature without being rushed?" she replied, her tone mock-indignant.

Marcel slowed to join her, a small smile playing on his lips. "You're right," he admitted. "It is beautiful. But we'll never make it to lunch if you keep stopping to admire every tree."

Genevieve rolled her eyes good-naturedly and nudged him with her ski pole. "Always practical, aren't you?"

"And that's why we make a good team," Marcel replied, his voice warm with affection.

Ahead, Jean-Pierre and Chantelle were navigating the twists and turns of the trail, their playful rivalry unabated.

"Watch out for that branch, Jean-Pierre," Chantelle called, narrowly avoiding a low-hanging limb herself.

"Thanks for the warning," he replied dryly, ducking just in time.

The trail eventually led to a small, rustic restaurant nestled in a clearing. Its wooden beams and stone chimney exuded a cosy charm, and smoke curled invitingly from the chimney. Inside, the family found a table near the window, which offered a stunning view of the surrounding peaks.

The warmth of the restaurant was a welcome reprieve from the cold, and the smell of hearty alpine dishes—cheese fondue, roasted potatoes, and cured meats—filled the air.

Marcel ordered a bottle of vintage wine, and the family settled into a lively conversation as they waited for their meal.

"So, let's hear it," Jean-Pierre said, leaning back in his chair. "Who was the most impressive on the slopes today?"

"Me, obviously," Chantelle said, her tone light but confident.

Jean-Pierre raised an eyebrow. "Really? I seem to recall someone almost taking out a tree."

"That was a tactical manoeuvre," she shot back, earning a laugh from both her parents.

Marcel held up a hand to restore order. "Let's settle this objectively," he said. "Genevieve, as the most graceful skier in the family, you decide."

Genevieve smiled, taking a sip of her wine before answering. "I think you were all equally entertaining," she said diplomatically. "But Marcel and I are still the reigning champions when it comes to elegance."

"Elegance doesn't count," Jean-Pierre muttered, though his grin betrayed his amusement.

As the meal progressed, the conversation turned to lighter topics, and the family's laughter filled the cosy space. Marcel shared stories from his early days as a physicist, recounting an ill-fated attempt to ski during a conference trip in Austria. "Let's just say the laws of physics weren't on my side that day," he said, drawing chuckles from the table.

Genevieve, not to be outdone, shared a tale from their first family ski trip, when Chantelle, then a fearless five-year-old, had attempted to race an entire group of teenagers down the slope. "She didn't win, but she certainly won their admiration," Genevieve said, smiling fondly at her daughter.

Chantelle blushed, but her eyes sparkled with the memory. "And Jean-Pierre was too busy building snow forts to even notice," she teased.

"I was perfecting my architecture skills," Jean-Pierre countered, feigning indignation.

The teasing continued as the meal wound down, the family's bond growing stronger with each shared memory and laugh. For a brief moment, the weight of recent events seemed far away, replaced by the simple joy of being together.

As they stepped back outside, the sun was beginning to dip behind the mountains, casting long shadows across the snow. The family lingered for a moment, taking in the breathtaking view.

"Days like this remind me why we work so hard," Marcel said quietly, his voice carrying a note of reflection. "It's for moments like these."

Genevieve slipped her arm through his, leaning against him. "And it's days like this that make it all worth it," she agreed.

Chantelle and Jean-Pierre stood a few steps ahead, their silhouettes outlined against the golden light. Jean-Pierre turned to his sister, his tone teasing but affectionate. "Think you can keep up on the way down?"

Chantelle grinned, her competitive spirit reignited. "Only if you don't cheat."

As the family prepared for one final run down the mountain, their laughter echoed through the trees, a testament to their resilience and love. Though challenges lay ahead, for now, they had each other—and that was enough.

Chapter 39

The setting sun bathed the vineyard in hues of amber and gold, casting long shadows over the rows of grapevines. The Dupont family had returned to their estate after a day on the slopes, their spirits high from the shared joy of skiing and the reconnection it had fostered. But now, as the evening settled in, a quiet contemplation filled the air. Each member of the family carried the weight of recent events differently, but all felt the profound shift in their lives and the world.

Inside the warmth of the Dupont manor, the family gathered in the expansive kitchen, their sanctuary and meeting ground. The large wooden table at the heart of the room, polished from years of use, was laden with a simple yet elegant dinner: roasted vegetables, fresh-baked bread, a fragrant herb-stuffed chicken, and a bottle of their finest vintage wine.

Chantelle sat at the table, her chin resting on her hand as she swirled the wine in her glass. The flames in the hearth crackled behind her, casting a warm glow on her thoughtful expression.

"These past months," she began, her voice soft but steady, "have been... overwhelming, to say the least. I've seen so much at the hospital—pain, desperation, but also resilience. And now, with the changes happening in the world, I feel like I've been given an opportunity to truly make a difference."

Marcel looked up from his plate, his deep gaze encouraging her to continue.

"At first, I doubted myself," Chantelle admitted, glancing at her father. "There were so many nights I lay awake, wondering if I was capable of being the doctor people needed. But seeing the drop in drug-related cases recently, it's like a weight has been lifted. I feel... hopeful. Like maybe we're finally turning a corner."

Jean-Pierre, seated across from her, nodded. "You're stronger than you give yourself credit for, Chantelle. You always have been."

Chantelle smiled faintly, her green eyes meeting her brother's. "I still have a lot to learn. But I think I'm ready for the challenge. I want to focus on preventative care—on educating people, especially younger patients, so they never have to end up in an emergency ward."

"That's a noble path," Genevieve said, her tone proud. "And I have no doubt you'll succeed. Your compassion is your greatest strength, darling."

As the conversation shifted, Genevieve leaned forward, her excitement evident as she addressed Jean-Pierre.

"I've been reflecting a lot on my work with preservation techniques," she said. "The past year has taught me some hard lessons about the importance of oversight and accountability. But it's also reignited my passion for innovation. I'm more determined than ever to refine our methods."

Jean-Pierre raised an eyebrow. "Refine how?"

"For one, I want to implement even stricter controls," Genevieve explained. "I've already started drafting new protocols for the winery. Every stage of the preservation process will have multiple checks, and I'm investing in more advanced equipment to ensure there's absolutely no room for error."

"And beyond the vineyard?" Marcel asked, his curiosity piqued.

Genevieve's eyes lit up. "I've been in touch with some colleagues about expanding these techniques into other industries—pharmaceuticals, food preservation, even humanitarian aid. Imagine if we could create safer, more efficient ways to store vaccines or preserve food in disaster zones. What happened with the contamination has taught me that science must always prioritise safety. But it's also reminded me of its power to create lasting change for the better."

Jean-Pierre smiled, his hazel eyes reflecting admiration. "That sounds ambitious, but if anyone can do it, it's you, *Maman*. You've never been one to shy away from a challenge."

Genevieve chuckled softly, reaching over to touch her son's hand. "And neither have you, my dear. Which brings me to another point—your role in all of this."

Jean-Pierre shifted in his chair, a flicker of surprise crossing his face. "My role?"

"Yes," Genevieve said firmly. "You've always been the grounding force in this family, Jean-Pierre. You're the one who ensures that what we've built—the vineyard, the winery, our legacy—remains intact. I've seen the way you've handled the challenges over the past months, and I couldn't be prouder."

Marcel nodded in agreement. "Your mother is right. You've proven yourself not just as a vintner but as a leader. It's clear that the future of this vineyard is in capable hands."

Jean-Pierre leaned back, his expression contemplative. "I've thought a lot about the responsibility I carry, especially recently. It's not just about maintaining the vineyard—it's about honouring the values you and *Maman* instilled in us: integrity, innovation, and family.

The challenges we've faced have reinforced how important those values are."

He paused, his gaze sweeping the room. "But I've also learned something else. The vineyard isn't just about tradition—it's about evolution. I want to explore more sustainable practices, new ways of working with the land that respects its history while ensuring its future."

Marcel's face softened, pride evident in his expression. "You've always had a vision, Jean-Pierre. And now, I see it's more than just a dream—it's a plan. Whatever path you choose, you'll have our full support."

The conversation turned to Marcel, who had been quietly observing the exchange. His deep voice broke the silence, carrying the weight of his thoughts.

"Everything we've been through—both as a family and as individuals—has taught me that no achievement, no discovery, is more important than the people we share it with. I've spent my life pursuing knowledge, driven by a need to understand the universe. But in doing so, I realise now that I sometimes lost sight of what truly matters."

He looked at Genevieve, his eyes softening. "You've been my anchor, Genevieve, through every triumph and every storm. And you, Jean-Pierre and Chantelle, you've given my life meaning beyond science or legacy."

Marcel paused, collecting his thoughts. "The lecture on gamma rays and supernovas I was preparing before all this—after what we've experienced, it feels different now. I used to see radiation as a force of destruction, but I'm beginning to understand it also as a force of transformation. It mirrors what we've gone through—our family, the world. Out of disruption, something new emerges."

Genevieve reached for his hand, her voice steady. "And that 'something new' is what we build together. As a family."

The room fell into a comfortable silence, the kind that comes when words have reached their limit. Each member of the family felt the profound shift in their dynamic, the unspoken acknowledgement of the lessons they had learned and the bonds they had strengthened.

Marcel poured more wine into their glasses, raising his in a toast. "To the future. To lessons learned and to building something even greater together."

The glasses clinked, the sound resonating in the warm, firelit room.

Chantelle smiled, her heart lighter than it had been in months. "And to us. To family."

As the evening stretched on, the Duponts shared stories, dreams, and plans, their laughter echoing through the manor. The vineyard outside, silent and waiting, seemed to hold its breath for the new chapter that lay ahead—one built on resilience, unity, and hope.

Chapter 40

The soft glow of the desk lamp cast long shadows across Marcel's observatory, a sanctuary perched atop the family's chateau. The observatory was a space that reflected the duality of his identity—a scientist and a dreamer. It was filled with shelves of books on astrophysics, vintage star maps, and sleek, modern equipment. The wide dome above opened to the heavens, revealing the vast night sky that Marcel had spent decades studying.

In one hand, he held a glass of his family's finest Pinot Noir, its rich aroma mingling with the faint scent of aged paper and polished metal. In the other, he swivelled the mouse and flipped through the slides of his upcoming presentation. The light from his computer screen illuminated his face, revealing the lines etched there by years of curiosity, dedication, and, most recently, the weight of extraordinary events.

Marcel's fingers hovered over the keyboard as he edited some notes and then continued to scroll through the slides. Each one detailed his research on gamma-ray bursts, supernovas, and the intricate dance of radiation in the universe. The presentation was technical, aimed at his peers in the scientific community, but tonight, after the family's heartfelt conversation, he felt compelled to infuse it with something more—something human.

His mind replayed Genevieve's passionate words about innovation and sustainability, Jean-Pierre's resolve to honour the past while embracing the future, and Chantelle's courage in the face of uncertainty. These weren't just lessons confined to their vineyard or family—they were universal.

Marcel paused on a slide illustrating a gamma-ray burst's destructive power. The diagram showed the intense energy released during a star's death, an event that could sterilize entire galaxies. He took a sip of wine, the liquid's warmth spreading through him, and thought of Genevieve's words:

Out of disruption, something new emerges.

He added a note beneath the slide:

"Radiation: A paradox of destruction and creation. Like humanity, it holds the capacity for both devastation and transformation. How we wield knowledge determines the outcome."

Moving to the next slide, he found a visual of a nebula—an ethereal cloud of gas and dust birthed from a supernova. It reminded him of Chantelle's journey, from doubt to confidence and how the family's crisis had pushed her to grow.

"From the ashes of destruction arises new life. A nebula is not just a graveyard of a star but a nursery for new worlds. In the same way, humanity can rebuild from its greatest crises."

Satisfied, Marcel leaned back in his chair and took another sip of wine. His presentation was evolving, no longer just a scientific lecture but a message of resilience and interconnectedness—a call to view science not in isolation but as a reflection of the human condition.

With the revisions complete, Marcel saved his work and turned his attention to the telescope, his most prized possession. It stood tall and sleek; its lens pointed skyward, a portal to the infinite. Marcel approached it with reverence, as though greeting an old friend.

The telescope had been with him through countless nights of discovery, a constant even as his life shifted. Tonight, it felt particularly significant. He adjusted the lens, aligning it with a section of the night sky teeming with stars.

The first sight that filled his viewfinder was Andromeda, its spiral arms stretching across the darkness. Marcel smiled faintly, remembering how he had once shown this galaxy to Chantelle and Jean-Pierre when they were children. Jean-Pierre had marvelled at its size, while Chantelle had asked why it wasn't crashing into them. He had explained patiently that Andromeda was billions of light-years away and that its collision with the Milky Way was far beyond their lifetime—a lesson in perspective that even now felt relevant.

Switching his focus, Marcel sought out a quasar, one of the brightest and most distant objects in the universe. Its light, he explained to himself, was ancient, a glimpse into a time when the cosmos was young.

"How small our crises seem against the backdrop of eternity,"

Marcel thought, yet he knew the weight of their actions rippled across time and space. Their recent ordeal had altered lives, rewritten stories, and, perhaps, changed the course of humanity.

Marcel stepped away from the telescope and walked out onto the adjacent balcony, his thoughts drifting as he gazed at the night sky unaided. The stars, brilliant and countless, seemed to whisper secrets of the universe. He took another sip of wine, savouring its complexity—a complexity mirrored in the cosmos.

He thought of the radioactive contamination that had thrown their lives into chaos, an accidental convergence of science and circumstance. The crisis had been a stark reminder of the double-edged sword that knowledge could be. Yet it also reaffirmed his belief in humanity's capacity to learn, adapt, and evolve.

Marcel's mind returned to his family, their resilience a testament to this belief. Genevieve's determination to turn a tragedy into progress, Jean-Pierre's unwavering commitment to preserving their legacy, and Chantelle's courage to embrace the unknown—all of it filled him with hope.

He raised his glass to the stars.

"To my family," he said softly. "And to the mysteries of the universe that bind us all."

Marcel's thoughts turned inward, reflecting on his legacy. He had spent a lifetime pursuing answers, yet the most profound discoveries had been within his own family. The vineyard, the winery, the observatory— they were more than just his achievements. They were symbols of unity, curiosity, and the delicate balance between tradition and innovation.

He thought of Jean-Pierre, who now carried the torch of the vineyard. His son's vision for sustainable practices was a reminder that progress didn't mean abandoning the past. Rather, it was about building upon it with care and foresight.

Marcel considered Genevieve's aspirations, her passion for preservation now tempered with a cautious respect for the power of science. She had taught him that innovation wasn't just about what could be done but what *should* be done.

And then there was Chantelle, standing at the threshold of her medical career. Marcel felt a surge of pride as he thought of her. She had faced the crisis with grace, emerging stronger and more determined. He knew she would carry their family's values into the world, touching lives in ways they could only imagine.

The night deepened, and Marcel found himself drawn back to his computer. He opened a new slide, inspired by the evening's reflections. On it, he wrote:

"The universe teaches us that nothing exists in isolation. Every star, every particle, is part of a greater whole. Humanity, too, is interconnected—our actions ripple outward, shaping worlds we may never see."

He added an image of a star cluster, its countless points of light, a metaphor for the interconnectedness of life.

Marcel leaned back, satisfied. His presentation was no longer just about gamma rays or radiation—it was about humanity's place in the cosmos. It was about the choices they made and the legacies they left behind.

As the clock struck midnight, Marcel stood by the window, looking out over the vineyard. The rows of vines, now dormant in the winter air, stretched into the distance. Above them, the stars continued their silent vigil.

He felt a profound sense of peace, a rare clarity that only the night and the stars could bring. With a final sip of wine, he whispered, "The universe holds its secrets, but it also holds its answers. And we—my family, humanity—are part of that story."

Satisfied, Marcel turned off the lights in the observatory and made his way downstairs.

The warmth of the chateau enveloped him as he descended, a reminder that while the universe was vast and unknowable, home was where meaning truly resided.

www.ingramcontent.com/pod-product-compliance
Lightning Source LLC
Chambersburg PA
CBHW051314190726
48290CB00001B/144